MINT TO BE

ALSO BY KATIE CICATELLI-KUC

PUMPKIN SPICE & EVERYTHING NICE

QUARANTINE: A LOVE STORY

GOING VIRAL: A SOCIALLY DISTANT LOVE STORY

MINT TO BE

Katie Cicatelli-Kuc

SCHOLASTIC INC.

ISBN 979-8-225-00324-1

10 9 8 7 6 5 4 3 2 1 25 26 27 28 29

Printed in the U.S.A. 40

First printing 2025

Book design by Stephanie Yang

Scholastic Inc., 557 Broadway, New York, NY 10012
Scholastic UK Ltd., Bosworth Avenue, Warwick, CV34 6UQ
Scholastic LTD, Unit 89E, Lagan Road, Dublin Industrial Estate, Glasnevin, Dublin 11HP5F

For safety or quality concerns, please contact:
UK web address - scholastic.co.uk.productinformation
EU web address - scholastic.ie/productinformation

TO ALL MY RESCUE PETS THAT I'VE BEEN LUCKY TO LOVE THROUGHOUT MY LIFE: CALLIE, PUZZLE, BEIJING, HAMPTON, ELLIOTT, MUSH, WAFFLES, AND TUNA; AND TO *ALL* RESCUE PETS, AND TO ALL THOSE WHO WORK TIRELESSLY TO SAVE THEM.

OCTOBER, LAST YEAR.

"Two peppermint hot chocolates!" Jo called, holding two steaming mugs.

Aiden had his eyes fixed on the roaring fire in the corner of the coffee shop, his mind a million miles away. Cup o' Jo was one of his favorite spots in the world, and where he did his best thinking.

"Two peppermint hot chocolates!" Jo repeated, louder this time.

"Oh, sorry," Aiden said, his attention snapping back to reality. "Those are mine, thank you!"

"Here you go," Jo said, handing him the mugs.

It was an unnecessary formality. There was only one other customer in the coffee shop, and Jo, the owner, had known Aiden most of his life. He was also a regular, so Jo knew his usual order by heart: two peppermint hot chocolates—one for him and one for his best friend, Emma.

Who was late. As usual.

"You know, you *could* try a different drink," Jo teased.

This wasn't the first time he'd had this conversation with Jo or the other baristas, so Aiden said the same thing he always did: "Maybe next time."

"I've heard that one before." Jo laughed. "I assume Emma is on her way?"

"No comment," Aiden said with a grin.

He picked a table close to the fireplace with a view overlooking the town square. The leaves from the maple trees—which just a few weeks ago were brilliant shades of yellow, orange, and red—now mostly lay on the ground, and the trees looked like they were missing their clothes. Aiden squinted and realized little flecks of snow were falling. Flurries at the end of October. Not unusual for Briar Glen this time of year, but a sad sign that fall would soon be over.

Aiden checked the time on his phone: 3:12. Emma was supposed to meet him here at three, just like she did every Friday. Well, "supposed to" in Emma time. She might have run into Mrs. Ryan, their English teacher, and started telling her about a novel she had just read. Or maybe she'd seen a beautiful tree on the walk over and was trying to remember its scientific name. Aiden smiled. Being on time was not Emma's strong suit, but it was also one of the things he liked about her best. Maybe not so much the being late part, but the things that captured her attention—the way she wanted to learn about everything and anything—fascinated him.

He felt his smile getting bigger, thinking about a few months ago when Emma had found an injured squirrel. Emma didn't have her driver's license yet, so she had called Aiden and asked if he could give her a ride somewhere. It wasn't until Emma got in the car holding a cardboard box that she told him where they were going—to a wildlife rehab center. The drive lasted only twenty minutes, but the squirrel, which Emma had named Polly, seemed to be feeling better and was making no secret of its unhappiness about being contained. Every time the box shook, Emma yelped, which made Aiden laugh, which made Emma laugh, which made the box shake even more. By the time they'd reached the center, their stomachs hurt from laughing.

In the days following, Emma had given Aiden updates on Polly, who was soon well enough to be released back into the wild, though Emma was sad to say goodbye. Months later, with earnestness in her big blue eyes, Emma still thought aloud about Polly.

Aiden shook his head, forcing himself to stop thinking about Emma's eyes. He checked his phone again (now 3:18), then rubbed his cold hands together. It was chilly by the window, so he walked over to the fireplace and stretched out his hands, trying to warm them. But he knew it was futile; his hands were always cold. It had become a bit of a joke between him and his family, and every year his Christmas stocking was filled with packets of hand warmers.

At 3:20, the bell above the front door chimed. Aiden knew just by how quickly the door opened that it was Emma. He turned, and there she was, her blue eyes sparkling. She was wearing her boots, which made her the same height as him.

"I'm so sorry I'm late!" Emma said breathlessly as she unzipped her puffy pink jacket.

Aiden shook his head. "No worries." He nodded toward the table, where their hot chocolates sat waiting for them.

Emma tugged off her jacket, plopped down in her chair, and wrapped her hands around her mug. She inhaled before taking a sip. "Still warm," she said, delighted.

"It better be." Aiden chuckled. "I ordered it extra hot."

"You know me too well." Emma put her drink down, her face suddenly more serious. "So the reason I'm late—"

Aiden raised his hand like he was in a classroom. "Ooh, ooh, can I guess? Pick me! Pick me!"

"Hmm . . ." Emma pretended she was looking around the room. "Yes, you there, in the front."

"Were you looking at the afternoon sunlight?"

"What sunlight would that be?" Emma and Aiden looked out the window. The stark trees stood against the gray cloudless sky. "Those poor shirtless trees," she said, shaking her head in mock sympathy.

"Should we knit them some leaf-shaped sweaters?" Aiden asked. "Oh! Is that why you're late? Were you knitting leaf-shaped sweaters for the trees?"

His hazel eyes were so innocent that Emma almost couldn't tell he was kidding.

Emma wrinkled her nose. "No, but that reminds me. Did I tell you I want to learn how to knit?"

"Like . . . ironically?"

"Huh? No! What would one ironically knit?"

"I dunno . . . a tiny iron . . . made out of yarn? A . . . *yiron*?"

"Seriously? That's the best you could do?"

"I'm sorry! It was the only joke I could think of."

"Luckily, I forgive you," Emma teased, patting his hand. They looked down at Emma's hand on Aiden's hand. Neither one of them breathed for a second. Finally, Emma picked up both his hands and rubbed them between her own. "You, my dear, have icicles for fingers."

Aiden's hands suddenly felt very, very warm.

He cleared his throat and pulled his hands away before Emma could tell that they were shaking. "So, knitting?"

"Oh, that was it—just that I was thinking about starting a knitting club at school. I want to add as many extracurriculars to my college applications as I can, and I figure they might as well be practical ones."

Aiden quirked an eyebrow at Emma. "And a knitting club is what you came up with?"

"It was just an idea. It seemed better than starting a kombucha club! Anyway, none of this is why I'm late."

Even though they'd known each other for ten years, Aiden still had trouble keeping up with Emma's trains of thought. Sometimes he wondered if she had trouble keeping up with them, too.

"Okay, I can't wait any longer!" She took a big gulp of her hot chocolate, then dug through her bag and pulled out a rumpled flier.

Aiden's heart beat faster as he read it:

EASTON ACADEMY

A PRESTIGIOUS BOARDING SCHOOL

LOCATED ON MANHATTAN'S UPPER EAST SIDE.

A PROGRAM SPECIALLY TAILORED FOR

HIGH SCHOOL FRESHMEN THROUGH SENIORS.

GET A HEAD START ON COLLEGE, ALL IN NEW YORK CITY!

There was a photo of a smiling teenage girl holding a stack of books. Under her it read: *Apply now during open enrollment.*

Aiden looked up at Emma, confused.

"Doesn't it sound *amazing*?" Emma asked. "I was meeting with Ms. Grant—that's why I'm late—and she was telling me about this boarding school in New York. I know it's bonkers, but she thinks it would really help with college admissions, and—"

"Boarding school?" Aiden asked, trying to keep his voice neutral.

"Yeah, to help prepare for college," Emma explained. "Living on your own and everything."

"Isn't that what *college* is for?"

"Among other things."

"We're only sophomores! And you can barely drive."

"So? I don't need to drive if I move to New York."

"Wait a minute . . . You're not really thinking about applying, are you?"

"I dunno, I just learned about it from the guidance counselor, and . . . hey!" Emma's eyes stopped sparkling as she narrowed them at Aiden. "Are you saying I couldn't get in?"

"No, no, not at all," Aiden said quickly. "Quite the opposite. You *would* get in. That's why I'm . . ." But when Aiden saw the look of confusion—or was it disappointment?—in Emma's eyes, he said, "Wow . . . New York City . . ."

"My number one dream place to live!"

"A dream," Aiden whispered, almost to himself.

"*Dream* isn't the right word, actually. Because I'm *going* to live there someday."

"I know, I know." Aiden sighed. "But this isn't like the time you wanted to drop out of high school and join the circus."

"That was an April Fools' joke! Have I ever told you how gullible you can be, Aiden Cooper-Gallo?"

"Have I ever told *you* how good of an actor you can be, Emma Sherman?"

"I could have seen the world! But if I get into this school, I could see the world, too. Like it would help me get into an Ivy, you know?"

"Yes, of course," Aiden said, still distracted. "But what's the rush? Briar Glen is pretty great, too. Can't we just . . . enjoy the time we have together?" he asked, gesturing around Cup o' Jo.

"Absolutely," Emma said. "But don't you want to travel, experience what it's like in *different* parts of the world?" She had that faraway look in her eyes that Aiden knew all too well.

Aiden shrugged. "Sure, someday."

"But why can't someday be tomorrow? Or today?" Emma persisted.

"Because we're in high school? And we have our whole—"

"Lives ahead of us, I know. But we have to *plan* those lives. Our futures aren't just going to fall into our laps."

"I mean, isn't that kind of the nature of time?" Aiden asked. "Time carries on, and things just kind of play out the way they're supposed to?"

Emma groaned, then smiled. "You're impossible, you know that?"

Aiden did a little theatrical half bow. "Why, thank you!" he said, smiling back. But his smile faded as he read the flier. "Boarding school . . ." He absent-mindedly took a sip of his hot chocolate, the peppermint tingling his lips.

"Plus," Emma continued between sips of her drink, "it'll drive Kerry bananas if I move to New York and she's in Boston."

"Maybe a silly sibling rivalry isn't the best reason to uproot your life?" Aiden said.

"Easy for you to say, Mr. Only Child. Have you ever had a perfect older sister? Did I mention that she's applying to law school?"

"You might have mentioned it a few times."

Emma exhaled, the breath puffing her bangs up off her

forehead. "Anyway, Kerry's not why I would apply to Easton Academy."

"I know," Aiden said. "I was just teasing you."

"I know that you know."

"I knew it!"

They both laughed. The conversation was starting to feel almost normal again.

But as Emma talked about acceptance rates, tuition assistance, and trains to and from New York, Aiden started to think about the reality of not being able to see Emma every day. Not being near her every day, feeling the warmth emanating from her body, like he was now. Not looking into her eyes, watching them sparkle when she got excited about something, like he was now. And if she was in New York, how would he ever be able to tell her what he'd been keeping a secret for far too long?

Not even Aiden's peppermint hot chocolate could warm the coldness that was taking over his body.

1

EMMA

The train rumbles over the tracks, past snowy hillsides. It's only a few minutes after five o'clock, but it's pitch-black outside, and it looks like it's been dark for hours. The last time I took this train, summer was just starting, and the sun shone the whole six-hour train ride from Briar Glen to Grand Central in New York.

I stare at my reflection in the window. I feel like I've changed just as much as the landscape. On my last train ride, I didn't really know much about Easton, how much I would love the school, or how challenging the academics would be. On my last train ride, I didn't know how much I'd miss Briar Glen. I didn't know Victoria, who introduced me to Sam, my now boyfriend, who's sleeping on my shoulder. On my last train ride, I didn't know where my friendship with Aiden stood.

Six months later and I'm still not sure where it stands.

I take out my phone and scroll through my texts. I hate how far down Aiden's name appears. Our last exchange is from almost a week ago, when he sent me a picture of Mackerel, his dog, sitting in the snow. I open the image, Mack with snow covering his entire furry black body, even his black snout. His left ear is sticking up, like it always does, and his tongue lolls from his mouth. I zoom in on his grinning doggy face, and I'm hit with another pang of homesickness. I thought the pangs would lessen the closer I got to Briar Glen, but they just seem to be intensifying with every mile.

I scroll through our other texts. One-word replies. Thumbs-up emojis. All after I left town without saying bye to him. I didn't even tell him I'd be coming home to Briar Glen for the holidays, and I certainly didn't tell him Sam was coming with me.

Because Aiden doesn't know Sam exists.

The train makes a sudden sharp turn and Sam is jostled awake.

He sits up and stretches his neck. "Sorry . . . was I snoring?" he asks, yawning so hard his brown eyes water.

"A little," I tease.

He checks his watch. "Just two more hours to go?"

I look at the time on my phone. It's still open to my texts with Aiden. "Yeah, sounds right."

He nods at my backpack, which is sitting unopened at my feet. "Did you get some work done?"

"Not yet," I say. "Dr. Caldwell said the paper isn't due until two weeks after break."

"Yeah, but she also said we should have at least an outline ready by the time classes start again."

He bumps his shoulder against mine, though, and we grin at each other.

I've never had homework over a holiday break before. Aiden could never; he used to freak out if we had homework over the weekend. I sigh at the memory.

"You okay?" Sam asks. "We have plenty of time to do the outline."

"No, it's not that. It's kind of unreal to be going home after so long," I say, trying to recover. "I've never been away from Briar Glen for more than a week or two. Last time I was home, everyone was wearing sandals and flip-flops. Now . . ." I look at my boots, a recent purchase that Victoria talked me into buying.

Sam nods contemplatively. "I know what you mean. Did I tell you I went to summer camp when I was little? Like the real deal, sleepaway camp in the woods."

I try to picture a little Sam in a little sun hat, sitting by a fire, roasting marshmallows for s'mores. The image is not crystallizing.

"I only did it once. My parents bribed me with an ice cream cone every day for a month before I'd agree to go."

"And?"

"Oh, it ended up being incredible. Like one of those classic camp things, campfires and swimming and ghost stories. There was this one story about a hitchhiker. Can you believe that was ever a thing? Just pulling over and letting some rando in your car?"

"What does this have to do with being away from New York?"

"My point!" He holds up a finger imperiously. "It was weird to go home after four weeks. New York smelled terrible—"

"It still does!"

"And there were just people, like everywhere. And there were hardly any trees, and it was loud, and I didn't have to sleep on a bunk bed, and there weren't any mosquitoes in the bathroom, and it was nice to be home. But it was definitely weird at first."

"Summer camp," I say, trying to match this preppy Sam next to me—who almost always wears a collared shirt—with a summer camp version of himself, but it's impossible. "If it was so great, why didn't you go back?"

"It was fun, but it was too . . . rustic. And my parents wanted to take a family vacation. There was one summer where we drove all the way to Wisconsin. Glad we didn't see any hitchhikers," he says, shuddering.

I turn to face him and brush his reddish hair away from his forehead. "You're cute."

Sam blushes. "I'm serious, though. I get it, how this must feel. Or at least, I sort of get it, and you can tell me the parts I don't understand."

"Thank you," I say, nudging his shoulder.

The bump knocks my phone off my lap but Sam grabs it before it hits the floor. He hands it to me, and the picture of Mackerel fills my screen.

"That's a good-looking pooch," he says. "You didn't tell me you have a dog."

"I don't . . . though sometimes he feels like my dog. He knows his way to my house! I can't even tell you how many times he's just showed up at my back door." I smile, thinking of all the times I opened my kitchen door to find him sitting there, grinning his doggy grin.

"Aw, sweet. Is he a stray?"

"Mackerel? No way, definitely not a stray. He belongs to—"

But I can't finish the sentence. Sam looks at me expectantly.

"A childhood friend," I say vaguely.

Sam, unbothered, nestles up next to me. "Can we go ice-skating? Briar Glen has a rink, right?"

Ice-skating is one of the many things Aiden and I used to do together. "Yeah, of course." I force myself to stop thinking about Aiden and change the subject. "But ice-skating is just one thing. Briar Glen is so magical this time of year. I can't wait to show you our town square and the huge Christmas tree, and the holiday market, and—oh!—the winter festival, with the sledding race!"

"You're adorable, you know that?" Sam says with a lighthearted laugh, and my mood soars. He checks his watch. "Think we'll be in by seven?"

"We're a few minutes behind schedule. Not bad, considering all the snow on the ground," I say. "And considering how crowded these trains are, how much stuff everyone has." I look up at his snowboard, which is stowed above us, then teasingly dig my elbow into his rib cage.

When Sam and I realized how close Briar Glen is to where his family skis and snowboards every winter, our parents had a long video chat, and they decided Sam could stay with me for a few days before their trip to the slopes.

But Sam doesn't seem to hear me. "I'm hungry."

"The food in the dining car isn't bad."

Sam raises an eyebrow skeptically. "Nope, I can't. I got food poisoning from train food three years ago. I still can't even really get close to salami. Plus, I kind of want to check out a Briar Glen restaurant. What's your favorite place?"

"That's easy—Cup o' Jo, especially this time of year. It's my favorite coffee shop. They have these Santa-shaped pancakes that I've been eating since I was a kid." But I stop myself from going on. I'm not ready for Cup o' Jo yet—not ready for Aiden.

"That's cute." Sam looks at me with his dark brown eyes. I take in his freckles, the reddish hair that always seems to be falling onto his forehead. I feel my body start to tingle. I will *not* think about Cup o' Jo. Or Aiden.

"We'll figure something out," he says.

There is so much to figure out.

Sam checks his watch again, then puts his head back on my shoulder.

I can't help but grin. My boyfriend has his head on my shoulder.

My *boyfriend*.

I go back to looking out the window and see my smile fade in the reflection. I'm bringing my boyfriend to Briar Glen, to my hometown.

The place I haven't been in six months. The place where I left my childhood best friend.

And I never even said goodbye.

2

AIDEN

"Aiden?" Dad calls from downstairs. "Do you know where your gloves are?"

I look at the pile of clothes in my laundry basket. It started off as clean clothes, then became kind-of-clean clothes, and now it's a bit of a jumble, mixed with my winter coat, my hat, my scarf—but not my gloves.

"I'll find them!" I shout back.

I sigh, looking around my messy room, stacks of sheet music falling off my desk, my acoustic guitar propped up against my dresser, the torn dog bed in one corner, where Mackerel is lying. My digging has woken him, and he looks at me, his left ear sticking up, so it seems like he's listening to what I have to say.

"You know, you're lucky you don't have to wear gloves."

I bend down to pet his head, but before I can even touch him, he's standing, leaning against my legs, his entire sixty pounds wiggling, and I sit on the ground, where he tries to crawl into my lap. He's part collie, part shepherd (we think), and even though we adopted him four years ago when he was two years old, he still thinks he's a puppy.

I scratch the white patch on Mack's chest and he starts licking my face. He has terrible breath, but I always let him. He's licking my forehead when my door opens.

Grandpa laughs. "Found your gloves," he says, waving them in his hand.

"Thanks." I slide Mack off my lap and wipe my face. "Where were they?"

"Dining room table," he says, handing them to me.

"What were they doing there?" I speculate out loud. A part of me wonders if I temporarily "lost" them on purpose, but I don't want to think about it.

Grandpa shrugs, and Mack just wags his tail.

I slide my gloves on, then pull on my coat, brushing black and white dog hair off me.

"Let's get going," Grandpa says, already halfway down the stairs. "Those lights aren't going to hang themselves up."

"C'mon, bud." I pat my leg and Mack follows close behind. Dad is already waiting at the bottom of the stairs, leash in hand. He snaps it onto Mack's collar, who is wiggling again.

"Have fun!" Mom says, walking in from the home office, holding the tattered record-keeping book that tracks Grandpa's woodworking sales. "These numbers aren't going to balance themselves, either!"

"I'm not sure I'd call it *fun*," I say. "It's freezing out there."

"Great! So we'll be done in no time," Dad says on his way to the mudroom.

"We can't break a Cooper-Gallo family tradition," Mom says, brushing the hair out of my eyes.

"We," I say, making little quotation marks with my fingers and laughing.

Mom's side of the family have all lived in Briar Glen their entire lives. My great-grandpa was a carpenter, and he passed down the trade. Grandpa took the craft one step further and started making things like sleds to sell at the local markets, which he's been doing for almost thirty years and has turned into a family business.

Along with the carpentry business, somewhere along the way (the story shifts depending on who you ask), my family also became responsible for the Briar Glen Christmas lights. We hang them around the light poles on Main Street, in the town square—basically anywhere and everywhere that needs Christmas lights. The only lights we don't hang are the ones on the Christmas tree, which is because of some (mostly) friendly rivalry with the Daley family that started before I was born.

We usually put up the lights on a day that isn't too painfully cold. Which is apparently today, even though the temperatures are still in the thirties.

"Where's Grandma?" Mom asks.

"In here!" Grandma shouts from the mudroom, poking her head around the corner. "I'm burning up. Let's go!"

"Ma, I told you that you were going to overheat," Mom says, crossing her arms.

Grandma ignores her daughter and takes the leash from Dad's hand. "If no one else in this family is going to get a move on—"

"Okay, okay," Dad says affectionately, putting a hand on her shoulder.

And finally, or not finally, Dad, my grandparents, Mackerel, and I head outside. As soon as I step on the front porch, the cold is an icy blast in my face that stings my eyes.

Our house is at the bottom of a hill, and we make a right turn, past other houses just like ours—colonials, Capes—adorned with lights and lawn decorations. The decorations range from plastic Santas and nutcrackers, to animatronic reindeer, to inflatable decorations, which include train sets, Grinches, and every Disney character ever created. Out of all of them, though, my favorite is the light-up Snoopy carrying a Christmas tree, a group of Woodstocks behind him.

Well, it *used* to be my favorite decoration.

Even though I'm wearing gloves, my hands still feel cold, and I instinctively rub them together, then feel annoyed again. When Emma gave me the gloves for Christmas last year, she swore they were supposed to be the warmest gloves on the planet. Whoever made them has never been to Briar Glen in December.

It's just a little after six, but it's been dark for so long already it feels like it's midnight, and the streets are quiet as we walk, my grandparents bickering about which years we used multicolored lights, Dad trying—and failing—to interject.

Grandma swings her arms as she talks, so I grab the leash from her hand. Mack looks up at me, smiling his happy dog smile.

In just a few minutes we're on Main Street, and then the town square, where Mayor Faustino is waiting for us by the Christmas tree, which sparkles with its own lights.

"Ah, if it isn't my favorite Christmas lights–decorating family!" she says, bending down to pet Mackerel.

"That's because we're your *only* Christmas lights–decorating family," Grandpa jokes.

"Exactly! Hanging the lights on the tree is just child's play for the Daleys," Grandma chimes in.

Mayor Faustino laughs and winks at me.

I never know how to return a wink.

"I'll leave you to it," she says, standing up and gesturing to the bins of lights awaiting us. I look around at the gazebo—a ladder already unfolded inside—the benches, the picnic tables, all of which will soon be adorned with our lights. It always overwhelms me at first, but it also always overwhelms me by how beautiful it turns out.

The mayor walks away, and Mackerel looks up. "I wish you had thumbs," I say to him, and he whines. Sometimes I think Mack understands me.

"Aiden!" Grandma calls like a drill sergeant. "You and I will take the square. We can meet up with your dad and grandpa later." She does not mess around when it comes to Christmas lights. I salute her, but she's already rummaging through the bins and doesn't notice. "See, I told you, multicolor lights, just like last year . . . here," she says, handing me a tangled mess of cords.

"Sit," I say to Mack. I wrap his leash around my belt loop, even though I know he's not going anywhere, and start to untangle the lights. Which is hard to do wearing thick gloves, but I'm determined.

Dad and Grandpa have already wandered away down Main Street, untangling the lights as they go. Grandma hunts through a bin and pulls out another string of lights, which she untangles in record time.

“I’m going to put these on the benches,” she says, walking away before I can respond.

“Well, it’s just you and me.” I look down at Mack again, who wags his tail like he wants to help.

“Aiden!”

I turn around at the sound of someone shouting my name, the Christmas lights still a big jumble in my hands.

And then I immediately want to turn back around again when I realize it’s Emma’s parents.

“H-hi!” I say as they approach. It comes out more as a surprised yelp.

“It’s wonderful to see you,” Mrs. Sherman says. She reaches out to hug me, which is hard to do while I’m holding all the lights.

Mackerel is up and wiggling. “Oh, and you too,” Mr. Sherman says, scratching Mack behind the ear that doesn’t stick up.

Then we all stand there for an awkward moment. “We’re just on our way to pick up some chocolate chips from the store,” Mrs. Sherman says. “We’re baking for the holiday party.”

“We bought two bags of chocolate chips and still ran out,” Mr. Sherman says, laughing like it’s the funniest thing in the world.

"Oh," I say. Then, remembering my manners: "What are you making?"

"Our usual chocolate chip brownies," she says.

"Right, of course." Their brownies really are the best brownies I've ever had, and I feel my mouth start to water just the tiniest bit.

It's quiet for a beat too long, until Mr. Sherman says, "We also made sugar cookies, chocolate-dipped pretzels, peanut butter blossoms, chocolate shortbread . . ." He's ticking them all off on his fingers, and I feel myself getting hungrier with every dessert he mentions. "I'm sure I'm forgetting something."

"Probably," Mrs. Sherman says, looking at her watch. "But we need to get going."

"Yes! We have to pick up Emma from the train station," Mr. Sherman explains.

"E-Emma?" I echo weakly, my mouth dry.

"Yes," he says, looking confused. "Didn't you know she was coming home today?"

I want to say, "I didn't know she was coming home *at all*," but I settle on, "No, maybe I forgot." I'm trying really, really hard to smile, but it's really, really hard to do.

"We miss you, Aiden," Mrs. Sherman says, looking into my eyes. "I almost feel like I sent two kids to boarding school!"

"Yeah, we haven't seen nearly enough of you since Emma left.

We miss having you around the house," Mr. Sherman adds. "And you, too," he says, nuzzling Mack's head.

Mack thumps his tail in response.

"I guess I've just been . . . busy with school . . . and stuff."

There's another beat of too-long silence until Mrs. Sherman says, "We can't wait to see you at our holiday party. It's been ages. You and Emma must have so much to catch up on!"

"Uh-huh," I say, wishing the conversation would end already.

"It'll give you a chance to meet her new beau, too," Mr. Sherman says, winking at me.

What?

This time I'm at even more of a loss on how to return a wink, so I just stand there, staring blankly. "Beau?"

"Boyfriend," Mrs. Sherman says, rolling her eyes and jabbing her husband.

"I know what you meant. I just . . . didn't know what you meant."

"Oh . . ." Mr. Sherman says, wearing the look of a man who's accidentally revealed a secret. "She didn't tell you about Sam?"

"No, she sure didn't."

"Really?" Mrs. Sherman says. "They started dating pretty soon after Emma moved to the city."

"Oh."

We stand there in more awkward silence, then Mrs. Sherman checks her watch one more time. "Well, we really better go. We don't want to be late. It was lovely to see you, Aiden."

"You too," I say, mustering up the energy to give her a half-hearted smile, and they walk away.

Just behind them I see the star atop the Christmas tree sparkle, as if it's winking at me—as if it's mocking me.

I really, really hate winks.

DECEMBER, ELEVEN YEARS AGO.

"Aiden! Why aren't you ready to go?"

Aiden's mom walked into his room, surveyed the stack of Legos he was building. Her face softened. "Don't you want to see the tree get lit? Santa Claus is going to be there!"

"Right, Santa," Aiden said, trying to sound enthusiastic.

"Grandma and Grandpa are already in the car."

Aiden looked wistfully at his Legos, then got up and followed his mom downstairs to the mudroom. He slid his feet into his winter boots, and his mom knelt to help him zip up his jacket, then plopped a hat on his head.

The drive to the town square parking lot was quick, but Aiden didn't want to leave the warm car. His dad and grandparents got out, carefully climbing over snowbanks.

His mom opened his car door. "You okay?"

"Fine!" Aiden said quickly.

"Okay," his mom said uncertainly. "If you want to leave, just—"

"I'm *fine*!"

His mom held his hand as they walked through the powdery snow. They heard singing, and the closer they walked to the town square, the louder the singing got. Then they rounded the corner, and his mom gasped. "Look at that tree! And the carolers! And all the lights!"

Aiden took in the town square, which had been completely transformed into a little winter wonderland, with Cup o' Jo's hot chocolate tent, carolers singing on the steps of the gazebo, and Santa's chair behind them. It was hard to believe that just a few months ago he and his parents had gotten ice cream and sat on these benches, which were now decorated in his family's Christmas lights.

His grandparents and dad were already at the tree, a blue spruce, and his grandma turned around. "Isn't it beautiful?" she asked.

Aiden nodded quietly.

His grandpa smiled. "I think it's bigger than last year's tre—"

"Aiden! Aiden! Aiden!" came a voice from behind them.

Emma, in a bright pink snowsuit, barreled toward him.

"You're here!" she squealed.

Aiden's dad laughed. "You must be Emma."

"Hi, Aiden's dad!" Emma said, bouncing on her toes.

Her mom and older sister, Kerry, appeared from around the corner.

"Emma!" her mom said, out of breath. "I told you not to run away from me!"

"Yeah, Mom freaked out," Kerry said without looking up, tapping away at her phone.

"But I saw Aiden!" Emma exclaimed.

Emma's mom turned to Aiden's parents. "Hi, I'm sorry, I'm Melanie Sherman. I hear our kids have become best buddies."

"Aiden never stops talking about Emma!" said Aiden's grandpa, laughing.

"Same!" Emma's mom laughed, too. "I'm surprised we haven't met before. Briar Glen is so small."

The adults launched into a boring grown-up conversation about where their houses were, how long they'd all been in Briar Glen, and Kerry stared at her phone. Emma looked at Aiden. Even though they'd been playing together almost every day since kindergarten had started, Aiden suddenly felt a little nervous seeing her.

But if Emma felt nervous at all, she hid it well. "It's so magical!" she said, gesturing to the scene around them.

Friends, neighbors, classmates—it felt like all of Briar Glen was there—everyone filled with holiday cheer. Aiden's usually serious doctor was wearing a Santa hat and laughing with someone, and they both held cups of hot chocolate.

"Hey, what are you going to ask Santa for?" Emma shouted over the local scout troop's rendition of "Jingle Bells."

At the mention of Santa, Aiden felt his hands start to sweat in his mittens. "I dunno. Maybe some Legos," he mumbled.

Emma turned to look at the carolers, who were singing "Frosty the Snowman." She sang along with them, which made all the grown-ups laugh. The carolers sang a few more songs, which Emma either danced to or sang to, and Aiden found himself swaying a bit to the music.

The scouts trudged off the stage, and Mayor Hawkins picked up the microphone.

"Thank you, Troop 1129!" he said, and everyone clapped. He waited for the applause to die down before continuing, "And now, without further ado, I think it's time to make this tree shine."

Aiden's grandma said something about the Daley family, but it was quickly drowned out by the applause, which was even louder this time. Mayor Hawkins led everyone in a countdown from ten. Aiden looked around at the excited faces—grown-ups, too—and felt goose bumps running up his arms.

When the mayor got to one, the massive Christmas tree lit up, and Aiden and Emma heard everyone gasp.

Emma grabbed Aiden's arm. "Oooh!"

After a few moments of *ooh*ing and *aah*ing, Emma's mom asked, "Aiden, Emma, can we get a picture of you guys in front of the tree?"

"Oh, that's a great idea," Aiden's mom said.

Emma slung her arm around Aiden's shoulders, and the parents and grandparents all said "Aww" as they took photos.

Aiden pulled away, feeling embarrassed, but Emma was simply delighted. He felt embarrassed and something else, because soon . . .

The mayor picked up the microphone again. "I think our special visitor is here!"

The crowd gasped again, and Aiden looked at all the bundled-up and excited faces of the kids around him. He had hoped maybe this year would be different. Maybe *he* wouldn't show up.

Applause erupted from the crowd as a Briar Glen fire truck from the 1950s came around the corner. Its ladder was decorated with Christmas lights, and sitting on top was Santa Claus.

Aiden could feel the color draining from his face.

Emma turned to him. "Santa!" she said, too excited to say anything else.

Aiden tried and failed to smile.

"All the kids, come on over and line up, and you can sit with

Santa and tell him what you want for Christmas!" Mayor Hawkins continued over the microphone.

Aiden's mom grabbed his hand. "Let's go get you guys in line. It's pretty crowded, so we'll meet you back here by the tree when you're done, okay?"

Aiden, in a daze, walked with his mom. Emma's mom was holding her hand, and every few steps Emma turned to look at him.

By the time they reached the gazebo, Aiden was shivering, and not from the cold. They were pretty far back in line, but Aiden could see Santa sitting in his big chair, laughing his jolly laugh, stroking his beard. Aiden quickly looked away.

"I'll be right back there, okay?" Aiden's mom said, gesturing to where they had just stood.

Aiden nodded, unable to speak.

Emma's mom and Aiden's mom walked away together, chatting about some Christmas movie Aiden was too little to watch.

Emma stood in front of Aiden, peering at the long line, and then turned to him. "Are you okay?" she asked.

Aiden tried to nod but he felt frozen in place.

"Ho, ho, ho!" Santa bellowed.

The line inched forward, and Aiden was getting closer to Santa. He was sweating now, and his eyes were full of terror.

"Oh!" Emma said. Then, more quietly, "Are you afraid of Santa?"

"No!" Aiden said.

"It's okay! My cousin Lily is eight, and she's still afraid of Santa."

"Really?"

"Yep." Emma looked around. "Here, follow me." She offered Aiden a mittened hand.

"But we're in line; don't you want to see Santa?" Aiden's words came out in a rush.

Emma shook her head. "Everyone knows the real Santa is at the mall. This guy is just a stand-in."

He hesitantly held on to Emma's pink mitten as she pulled him out of line and guided him through the groups of kids waiting to see Santa. She stopped and let go of Aiden's hand when they got to the Cup o' Jo tent.

Jo was working, and her daughter, Lucy, who was a few years older than Aiden and Emma, was dutifully stacking a pile of paper napkins, which was a little hard in her thick gloves.

"One peppermint hot chocolate, please!" Emma said to Jo. "Hold the marshmallows."

"Ah, shoot," Jo said. "I just ran out of peppermint hot chocolate."

"No worries, you can do the trick!" Lucy said to Emma, taking a break from her napkins. “My mom showed you, right? Do you have a candy cane?”

Emma thought for a minute and then nodded eagerly.

“Perfect!” Lucy said.

Jo poured hot chocolate into a cup and handed it to Emma. “Careful now, it’s hot.”

Emma solemnly held on to the cup and walked a few steps to one of the picnic benches. The snow had been cleared away, and Emma set the drink down carefully.

Aiden approached the table and looked at the hot chocolate skeptically. “What are you—”

Emma held up a hand and reached into her snowsuit, tongue out in concentration as she dug around in her pockets. “Ah-ha!” she said, producing a wrapped candy cane.

“Why do you have a candy cane in your snowsuit?” Aiden asked.

“Why not?” Emma took off her mittens and quickly unwrapped the candy cane. Then, before Aiden even realized what she was doing, Emma stuck the candy cane into the drink and began stirring, her brow furrowed. After a minute, she handed the drink to Aiden, candy cane still poking out.

Aiden peered into the drink. “Why did you put candy in my hot chocolate?”

"Try it! Jo showed me," Emma said, sliding the drink into his hands.

Aiden held the drink, looking at it suspiciously. He sniffed the hot chocolate. It smelled pretty good. He took a careful sip. The chocolate mixed with the mint in the candy cane, and it tasted like a candy bar.

The most delicious candy bar.

He gaped at Emma in astonishment. "This is amazing!"

"Told you!"

But Aiden was too busy drinking to say anything back. They stayed at the table, Aiden gulping his peppermint hot chocolate, while Emma watched him, and smiled.

3

EMMA

"Next stop, Briar Glen!" a conductor announces as he passes through the train car. "Briar Glen, next stop!"

Next stop, I think. *How is this possible? Why can't it be a million more stops?*

Sam squeezes my hand. "Can't wait!"

"Me too." It's only a partial lie.

As the train slows down, Sam is already standing up, grabbing his duffel bag and snowboard off the luggage rack, then my suitcase.

He puts out his hand for me. "You ready?"

"I am!" I say quickly. Only another partial lie.

I grab the handle of my case and tug it. Just before we get to the door, Sam stops so I can step off the train first. "After you," he says. "It's your turn to show me around for once."

My turn, I think stepping off the train, Sam walking behind me. He's been the one showing me around the city ever since I left Briar Glen, taking me to all his favorite places. Now I'll be the one playing tour guide. I've never had to show anyone around Briar Glen before. Everyone has always just . . . been here.

I don't have time to think about it much more, though, because I see my parents on the train platform and start running toward them. "Mom! Dad!"

"Emma!" they both say. I don't know who to hug first, so I hug them both at the same time. My mom's hat tickles my cheek, and she smells like she always has. A mix of her vanilla lotion and . . .

Home. She smells like home.

I pull away, and I have tears in my eyes, and my parents are a little misty-eyed, too. "We've missed you so much!" my mom says, stroking my hair, then giving me another hug.

When we let go, I remember that Sam is standing behind me, smiling politely. "Oh my gosh! I'm sorry! Duh! Here is Sam!"

"Sam, it is so nice to meet you in person!" My mom pulls him into a hug, and it's so strange to see two separate parts of my life come together. Is this why I was feeling uneasy before? "We have heard so much about you!"

"Mom!" I say, suddenly embarrassed.

"All good things, I hope?" Sam says in his easy way as he pulls away from her.

"All excellent things," my dad says. "Let's hope they're all true." He sticks out his hand to shake Sam's hand. Sam's face pales for just a second, but then my dad starts laughing. "Just messing with you!"

"Dad!" I say, even more embarrassed.

"What! He's your first boyfriend. It's my job as your parent to grill him. And possibly embarrass you along the way," he says, waggling his eyebrows.

"I am *so* sorry," I say turning to Sam, but he's just laughing.

"Don't sweat it," he says. "Besides, your dad is right. He's *supposed* to embarrass you. I hope you have the old photo albums out! I'm ready to see any and all embarrassing pictures of Emma."

I look at my dad in horror, who is absolutely delighted. "Oh, just wait until you see her dance recital pictures. When she was three or four, she had this tutu, I swear it was the size of—"

"Hey, guys, I'm freezing," I interrupt. "Can we go to the car?"

"Of course, honey," my mom says, before my dad can continue his sentence.

My dad picks up my suitcase, then leads the way across the platform and down the steps to the parking lot.

"I am so sorry about that," I say to Sam as we walk.

Sam seems confused. "What? Your parents are great."

"I know," I say, thinking back to the first time I met Sam's parents.

They live close to Easton, in a sleek modern apartment. We drank sparkling water and ate flaky croissants that Sam's dad had picked up from their local bakery and talked about the trip to Toronto that they were planning. When I was done eating, after I brought my plate to the kitchen, I saw Sam's mom wiping away the croissant crumbs I'd left on the table.

"My parents are just . . . different," I finally say.

"Different isn't a bad thing."

My dad pops open the trunk of the car and slides in my suitcase and Sam's duffel bag and snowboard. My mom opens the back door for herself.

"Um, Mom?" I say, nodding at Sam.

She laughs. "Sorry! After Kerry moved out of the house, Emma liked me to sit in the back seat with her."

"Not all the time!" I say, that feeling of embarrassment returning.

My mom gets into her passenger seat, though, so I slip into the back seat with Sam. There is a mix of snow salt and dirt on the floor. I feel self-conscious about the mess, but Sam doesn't seem to notice.

We pull out of the train station, and as we turn onto Main Street any of my previous embarrassment fades.

"Ooh, this is where Kerry took lessons for years . . . and I did for a little bit," I say, pointing out the window at the dance studio.

"Why did you stop?" Sam asks.

"I just wasn't into it anymore." He doesn't need to know that I stopped in fourth grade, when I was cast as one of the rats in the *Nutcracker* recital. My sister, years before, had been Clara, which anyone and everyone liked to tell me.

"Oh, and here's where we took piano lessons," I say, pointing again. "I only played for a few years. I quit that in fourth grade, too."

I think about Kerry, who took lessons from when she was four until she graduated from high school and even minored in music theory in college.

"Smart. My parents made me take piano lessons until I was thirteen, but I really didn't like it."

"And you still regret quitting, right?" my mom pipes up from the front seat, turning around to face us.

Sam laughs. "Yes, Mrs. Sherman. I should have stuck with it. Just like Emma should have stuck with it."

"Traitor," I mouth to Sam.

"Sorry," he mouths back.

My mom turns around again, and she gives my dad a little satisfied smile.

Sam takes his phone out and starts scrolling.

"Sam!" I say, but it comes out much sharper than I intend, and he's startled. My dad looks at me from the rearview mirror. "It's just . . . don't you want to see downtown Briar Glen?"

I point out the light poles adorned with Christmas lights. I start to wonder when Aiden and his family put them up, if the gloves I gave him kept his hands warm, but I push the thoughts out of my mind.

"Oh, sure," Sam says. "Sorry, was just reading something from Dr. Caldwell about the outline."

My dad slows down, and I point out our pharmacy, the local hardware store, the library, all adorned with wreaths and window decorations. We pass more light poles with Christmas lights strung up on them, but I try not to look.

"I love it," Sam says, facing me. He starts to reach for his phone in his pocket again, but then grabs my hand instead, squeezing it. "Thank you for bringing me to Briar Glen. This means a lot to me."

I squeeze back, calling out more storefronts.

"How does the town square look?" I ask my parents. It's at the other end of town from the train station, and we could drive past it on a roundabout way to our house.

"Gorgeous as always," my mom says.

"They say the tree is the biggest one they've had," my dad says.

I laugh. "They say that every year! Don't drive by it now, though, okay? I want to walk there with Sam."

My dad nods. "Roger that."

I start to roll my eyes, but grin at Sam.

Sam catches me looking at him. "What?"

"Nothing! I'm just happy."

"So am I," he says, looking into my eyes. He leans forward like he's about to kiss me, but my dad drives over a pothole, and Sam and I bounce away from each other.

"Whoops! Sorry about that!" my dad says sweetly.

"Funny, Dad," I say, refusing to succumb to embarrassment. Again.

We pull up to my house, and I hear a gasp, and then realize it's mine.

My little blue craftsman house has lights strung across its entire front porch, from the railings on the stairs to the posts, to the ceiling overhead. The lights twinkle at me in blue and red and orange and green. There's a huge wreath hanging from the front door. The old Santa and reindeer that were my mom's when she was little are in our front lawn. Plastic candy canes line the path up to the porch. There is just a little bit of snow on the ground.

"You guys aren't joking with your decorations," Sam says.

But his words barely register as I climb out of the car, taking it all in. Through the front window, I can see the tree in the living room, lit up and decorated.

This is the first year I haven't helped my parents decorate the tree. Tears spring back into my eyes again, but I quickly brush them away. My mom examines my face.

"It's the cold, dry air!" I say.

"There seems to be a lot of it." My mom dabs at her own eyes, then wraps her arm around me in a sideways hug. "I'm so happy you're here!"

I look at Sam looking at my house and say, "I am, too."

My parents walk up the pathway and porch, and the front door creaks open.

Sam tugs at my hand. "I could really use a bathroom. Ready to go inside?"

"Yeah, sorry," I say, snapping out of the trance I was just in.

As soon as we step inside, I'm enveloped in the smell of baking sugar cookies. I stand in our narrow entryway, looking at the garland wrapping up and around the staircase railing. I peer around the corner at the scene of little holiday houses set up on a table in our living room. The snow globe on the coffee table. And, of course, the tree.

Its white lights shimmer at me, and I see all our ornaments. The little Baby's First Christmas ornaments for my sister and me; the penguin ornaments, something my sister collected when she was little; and all the Snoopy ornaments, my collection.

All decorated without me.

"I'm so sorry we didn't wait for you to decorate the tree!" my mom says as she removes her boots.

"No, it's okay." I smile weakly.

I look at the tree again, and I don't know how I missed it, but there is the wooden sled ornament, made by Aiden's grandpa.

I tear my watery eyes away from the tree. Sam has taken off his coat, and my dad hangs it for him on our overflowing coat rack.

Sam looks at his boots. "Where should I . . ." He trails off when he sees the overcrowded shoe mat.

"Oh, anywhere is fine," I say. I take the boots from his hand and toss them on top of my boots. "C'mon, I'll give you a tour!"

My parents are in the dining room. My mom has decorated the table with her little winter landscape of a snowy-white squirrel wearing a Christmas hat, a reindeer candle sconce, and another handcrafted mini sled. There's a red and green tablecloth, with a just-visible stain from when I spit out fruitcake that I insisted on trying when I was ten.

It's a small room. I try to see it from Sam's eyes, wonder if he sees the clutter of papers on one corner of the table.

"Um, this is the dining room," I say, gesturing around me.

Sam nods, the obedient guest on my tour. I take his hand and bring him into the living room, which is also connected to our entryway. There's the fireplace with our four stockings hanging from the mantle; the Mr. and Mrs. Claus pillows on the couch, which we've had ever since I can remember; the winter Snoopy and penguin figurines all over our bookshelf, which long ago ran out of room for books, so now the newer books are haphazardly stacked on top of one another.

But Sam is touching the tree, looking at it in admiration. "Is this real?" he asks, inhaling deeply.

"It is!" I say proudly.

"I've never had a real tree," Sam says, still smelling. "My parents always said the needles were too messy."

"Your parents might be on to something." I turn around, and it's my sister, Kerry. "Mom gets so stressed about the needles," she says by way of greeting as she gives me a hug. Kerry is eight years older than me, and almost a foot taller. Her hair, in a neat ponytail, brushes against my face as she lets me go.

"Hello to you, too," I say, laughing.

"I was on cookie duty."

The sugar cookies. Another thing I used to do with my family.

"Mom wanted it to smell nice when you walked in the door," Kerry says.

It should make me feel better, but I feel another twinge of sadness.

"And this, I assume, is the infamous Sam," Kerry says, crossing her arms and peering at my boyfriend.

"I prefer famous, but we can stick with infamous for now." Sam smiles and extends his hand to my sister. "I was one of the flying monkeys when my elementary school put on a production of *The Wizard of Oz*. But I don't want to brag."

"A handshake. I like it," Kerry says approvingly.

"I learned to shake hands before I could walk."

"Emma, you didn't tell me your boyfriend was a comedian," Kerry stage-whispers at me.

"Aaaand that's enough of that!" I say, taking Sam's hand again, walking him through the entryway, back into the dining room. "This is the kitchen, obviously," I say, bringing him into our small galley-style kitchen.

The oven is on, and the smell of baking sugar cookies escapes it. There are piles of tin-foiled plates and Tupperware containers scattered around the counters. I forgot how messy our house gets during the holidays.

"Sorry, we may have all gotten a little carried away with our baking," my mom says from the dining room, where she's sitting, fiddling with a snowflake napkin holder. "We'll get dinner started. How about your favorite macaroni and cheese?"

My stomach grumbles.

"We've been so busy getting ready for the party!" she goes on. "There are sugar cookies, peanut butter blossom cookies, maple cheesecake, chocolate-covered pretzels, chocolate chip brownies, peppermint brownies—"

I hear myself inhale sharply at the word *peppermint*.

"Whoo! Let's get out of the kitchen! It's hot in here," I say, fanning myself.

"Yeah, but . . . it's kinda nice after the cold outside?" Sam says uncertainly.

And then I remember: "Bathroom! I'm so sorry; I forgot to show you the bathroom. Follow me."

Sam follows me to the upstairs bathroom, and then I show him the three bedrooms upstairs, including the guest room, where he'll be staying.

"And this is it," I say, standing in my room. The trundle under my bed has been pulled out for Kerry, and her suitcase is in the closet, but other than that, the room looks like nothing in it has moved in months. Which is probably really the case, I realize.

"And this is it," Sam repeats quietly as he gazes around my room.

I'm struck again by the strangeness that my boyfriend from New York is standing in my childhood bedroom in Briar Glen.

I try to see this room through his eyes, too. I think again about meeting his parents. He didn't even have a room at the apartment, just a loft space with a bed he said his parents had bought recently.

My bed, which is still made up with the same sheets and patchwork quilt that I've had since I was little. The pale blue walls that my mom, dad, and I painted in eighth grade to finally cover up the bright yellow I picked out when I was four. My built-in bookcase, the books neatly lined up; my dresser, the top empty except for a jewelry box and a small bin of stuffies. There's a bulletin board: my acceptance letter from Easton Academy pinned front and center; fortunes from fortune cookies I've collected over the years; a ticket stub from a concert Aiden and I went to . . . and a picture Aiden drew for me when we were in kindergarten.

"Who drew the picture?" Sam asks. "One of your younger cousins?"

"Oh . . . yeah. Something like that."

"Aw, it's so sweet that you kept this." Sam points to the acceptance letter.

"Sweet that I'm proud of my academic achievement?" It comes out with less humor than I hoped. "Sorry, I think I'm getting a little hangry?"

"I was so busy taking in all this Emma I almost forgot I was hungry."

"All this Emma?" I ask, confused.

Sam puts his arms around me. "Yes. This is you. This is Emma. Your origin story."

My heart is beating so loudly I can feel it throughout my entire body. I look into his brown eyes, and he's just about to kiss me when I hear coughing. I pull away from Sam abruptly and turn to see Kerry standing at my bedroom door, hands on her hips.

"Sorry to interrupt you two lovebirds," she says, smirking.

I feel my face flush in embarrassment, especially at the word *love*. Something Sam and I haven't said to each other yet. I wonder if we ever will.

Sam doesn't miss a beat. "Emma and I were just saying that maybe we could order some food," he says, looking from me to my sister.

Kerry snorts. "Good luck this late in the day."

Sam checks his watch, and then looks at me. "It's not even eight."

"We're a sleepy little town," Kerry says. "But if you really want to go out, what about Cup o' Jo? She stays open later this time of year. Emma, you could get your Santa pancakes! And maybe you'll run into—"

"No!" I'm not ready for Aiden yet.

Kerry studies my face. Sam gives me a curious look.

I'm still thinking of what to say when I hear my parents' footsteps on the stairs. "Why didn't anyone tell me sooner that this is where the party is?" my dad asks, popping his head into the room.

"Daaaad," Kerry and I groan.

My mom rolls her eyes at him, but there's a faint smile on her face. "Dinner shouldn't take too long. Why don't you get settled and wash up?"

"Actually," Sam begins, "we were just saying we might go out for a quick bite? I can't wait for Emma to show me more of Briar Glen! And I didn't want to trouble you. I'm sorry. I should have asked first."

"It's no trouble," my mom insists. "But if you want to show Sam around Briar Glen, Emma . . ."

The room is quiet as everyone looks at me. I love my mom's macaroni and cheese, and as much as I missed Cup o' Jo, I'm not sure I'm ready to go there just yet. But Sam looks at me hopefully, and I think about my Emma origin story, and I hear myself weakly saying "Santa pancakes."

"Cup o' Jo!" my mom says. "Maybe you'll see—"

"I think we should get going!" I interrupt. "Are you ready, Sam?"

I start walking down the stairs before he has a chance to answer me, or before anyone else has a chance to hint about Aiden.

"Enjoy," my mom says. "And say hi to Jo for me!"

"Will do!" I say, pulling on my coat and boots.

Sam and I head out the door, and I walk fast, trying to focus on my favorite Christmas decorations, and not the lurch in my stomach I felt every time someone in my family almost said Aiden's name.

I show Sam my favorite decorations. "Isn't that Snoopy with all the Woodstocks adorable?"

"*You're* adorable," Sam says, squeezing my hand.

I feel a goofy grin spread across my face as we keep walking, and the uncomfortable feelings start to fade as we get to the town square. The tree shimmers and shines at me, and as much as I want to ignore the Christmas lights, it's hard to when they've been strung from the gazebo, the benches, and the light poles. And they look perfect.

Aiden.

"Pretty incredible, isn't it?" I ask, shaking away the thought.

"It's beautiful," Sam says quietly. He wraps an arm around my shoulder. "Just like you."

I elbow him. "Cheeseball."

Sam laughs, kissing my forehead.

Just off the town square is Cup o' Jo, its windows glowing warmly against the dark winter night. And even though I'm happy to be back, I feel a twinge of disappointment and maybe even panic at the thought of going inside. "You don't want to just . . . stand here a little bit longer?"

"Wait, is that . . . is that a Java Junction?" Sam asks, squinting at the storefront across from Cup o' Jo.

"Yeah, so annoying that they opened," I say distractedly. "We—I mean, I—am pretty loyal to Cup o' Jo."

But Sam doesn't hear me as he pulls his phone out of his pocket. He taps a few times and then says, "Perfect!" He looks up at me. "I'm going to run over and pick up my order."

"Your order?"

"I needed a quick snack. A pumpkin spice latte and one of the mini pecan pies. Just enough to tide me over until a proper dinner."

"But . . . we're literally about to go in."

"Two minutes! I'll just be two minutes!" he says, already walking away. "I'll meet you inside."

"Okay?" I say uncertainly.

I watch him go into Java Junction, and I turn back to Cup o' Jo, its windows covered in hand-drawn penguins, snowflakes, a menorah, Christmas trees, and Santas. Just before I open the door, a rush of Aiden memories pushes its way into my head. I squeeze my eyes shut, keeping the memories out, trying to think about Santa-shaped pancakes and keeping Aiden-shaped memories out of my mind.

I take a deep breath. The bell jingles as I open the door. I've missed that familiar chime.

My sixth-grade science teacher sits at one of the tables, and a group of out-of-towners is at another. Jo is behind the counter, making a coffee, and Lucy is at the register, where a customer pays for an order. Lucy hands the customer their receipt, then sees me and does a double take.

"Emma!" she says, walking around the counter and giving me a hug. "I didn't know you were in town!"

"I just got here!" I say. "I didn't know you were here, either!" Lucy and her boyfriend, Jack, go to college together a few hours away.

"Winter break. Thought Mom could use some help," she says, nodding over her shoulder.

Jo rings up a coffee order but grins at me. Finally, she steps away from the counter and wraps me in a big hug, saying, "It is so good to see you!"

She smells like coffee beans. Just like my mom's vanilla scent, it reminds me of home.

"It's so good to *be* here!" But I don't know how much I really mean that.

"You look different," Jo says, pulling back from our hug, inspecting my face.

"I do?" I didn't realize my changes were visible.

Lucy peers at me. "I don't see it?"

"It's a mom thing," Jo says, holding my face in her hands.

I gaze around the shop. The shelf of books on one wall. The fireplace crackling in one corner. I think of all the times Aiden and I sat by that fire, the first time I talked about Easton by that fire. The same chairs and tables, all of which I've sat at with Aiden.

"Well, the shop looks exactly the same," I say. "In a good way!" I feel uncertain and nervous, which is an odd way to feel at Cup o' Jo.

Jo smiles warmly. "Good. We always want it to feel like home here."

"Home," I echo.

"Your parents said something about a boyfriend coming with you?" Jo asks.

"Mom! Don't be nosy!" Lucy says.

Just then, the bell jingles, and Sam walks in. To my horror he's carrying a Java Junction bag and coffee cup. "And here he is!" I say.

"I'm feeling much better now." Sam walks over and puts an arm around me. "Why didn't you tell me there was a Java Junction here, Emma? And—oh, I'm sorry, I'm Sam," he says to Lucy and Jo.

I look from Jo, who is mildly amused, to Lucy, who is mildly annoyed.

Sam's face reddens a bit when Jo and Lucy don't say anything.

"This is Jo, the Cup o' Jo owner, and this is Lucy, her daughter," I say quickly. "There was kind of a . . . rivalry between Java Junction and Cup o' Jo. A lot of us weren't happy when Java Junction moved in across the street."

I gesture around the shop, thinking this will be all Sam needs to see to realize what an injustice he's just committed, but he says, "Oh, I'm really sorry. This place is great! Very cozy."

"That's kinda our thing," Lucy says frostily. "Why go to Java Junction, a place you can go to anywhere, when you're in Briar Glen?"

Sam's face reddens more, and Jo says, "Lucy, why don't you get back to the counter? You know this lull won't last long."

"Gladly," Lucy says, giving Sam one final glare.

"Don't mind her," Jo insists. "It's still a sore spot for her sometimes. Anyway, go get comfortable, and I'll be back in a minute to take your order."

"Sure," I say. It's weird that Jo is explaining this all to us, like I haven't ordered from her a million times before.

"Thank you," Sam says as Jo goes back to the counter.

Sam points to a table by the window, but I shake my head. "Too drafty."

"By the fireplace?"

It makes me think of Aiden and Easton, so I shake my head again.

I look around the coffee shop. No table is safe. I've sat at every single one with Aiden.

"O . . . kaaay," Sam says. "Why don't you pick where to sit, then?"

I'm being silly. Just because Aiden and I used to hang out here all the time doesn't mean I can't be here now with Sam. "Let's sit here," I say, pulling out a chair at a table, trying to keep Aiden and all my Aiden memories out of my mind.

"Sure." Sam sits down, looking grateful.

Jo comes over to our table a few seconds later, beaming. "Emma, I can't tell you how wonderful it is to see you in here again. The shop has felt funny without you and Aiden."

"He hasn't been here?" I ask, hoping my voice is calm and measured.

Jo shakes her head, then takes in Sam.

"How did you two meet, anyway?" Jo asks.

Sam glances at me, suddenly shy again, and I say, "He was studying with my roommate, Victoria, for trigonometry—"

"I'm terrible at math," Sam interrupts, then looks at me. "Sorry, you were saying."

"I was in the kitchen, getting a snack. I saw him sitting there with Victoria, and realized they could use some help, so I helped, and then I guess we just started talking, and that was kind of it?"

Sam and I had ended up talking for hours that day. He was so different than Aiden. He loved school just as much as me. He had traveled all over the world. Sam told me about all his favorite restaurants in the city, and the day after we met, he took me out to his favorite boba tea spot, and he gave me a quick bashful peck outside my dorm room. It was my first kiss. The first of many. After that, we saw each other pretty much every day. As different as we were from each other, it felt seamless.

"It's more exciting than that, Emma!" he chimes in.

"No, no, I get it," Jo says. "It was easy, right, Emma?"

"Yeah." But I just want the conversation to be over. Seeing Sam sitting here is another collision between two of my worlds.

Jo seems like she's waiting for me to say more. "Sam and his parents ski a few hours north of Briar Glen, so we all thought he could come stay with us for a few days before meeting up with his parents. You know what Briar Glen is like this time of year!" As I speak, I feel some of my enthusiasm returning.

My boyfriend is in my hometown. My boyfriend wants to know my origin story.

"Of course! Most beautiful place in the world this time of year," Jo says. "But enough of me being nosy! What can I get you guys?"

"Emma has been telling me about these Santa pancakes, so she's getting those," Sam says.

"Is she?" Jo looks at me questioningly.

Something is off.

Sam has ordered for me in the city, when he's taken me to a restaurant he's been to before. But him ordering for me at Cup o' Jo feels all kinds of wrong.

"Yes, I'd like Santa pancakes," I say, looking at Jo. "Sam is right. And a peppermint—"

"Hot chocolate?" Jo says, grinning at me.

"Mocha," Sam and I say at the same time.

"Really?" Jo asks.

"I studied a lot at night at Easton and needed the caffeine," I say lamely. "But you know, I'll skip the hot drink. Just water for me. And pancakes."

Jo looks at me curiously—I've never been to Cup o' Jo and not gotten a peppermint hot chocolate—but I nod.

"And for you?" Jo asks, turning to Sam. "I don't know if you saw our specials, but we have a Thanksgiving leftover turkey sandwich, a Christmas ham sandwich, a breakfast sandwich, grilled cheese—"

"Okay, I'll take a grilled cheese sandwich, please."

"You sure?" I ask, feeling disappointed again. "The holiday specials are really good."

"No thanks. I'll just stick with the grilled cheese," he says.

"You got it," Jo says somewhat tersely and walks away.

Everything still feels off, but I ask Sam about the *Planet Earth* series he's been watching, and soon Jo brings us our food.

It almost feels normal. Except that I'm with Sam.

"This is really good," Sam says, taking huge bites of his sandwich. He looks around again. "I can see why this was one of your hangout spots when you lived here."

Was.

"I *do* still live here," I say.

Sam glances at me skeptically, then looks outside. "It's snowing!" I'm still processing him referencing Cup o' Jo in the past tense when he says, "I'd love to walk through a snowfall with you."

My heart flutters, and I remember again: *My boyfriend is with me in Briar Glen.* "Me too," I say. "I'm ready to go."

Jo is busy in the little kitchenette making a sandwich, and Lucy has a long line of customers, so I pay quickly, giving them both a quick goodbye wave.

Sam and I push open the door, and as we step onto the sidewalk the snowflakes land gently on us. Sam puts out his hand. The snowflake in his hand is huge, and I can see all its unique edges and angles.

We peer at it together. I feel my lips getting closer to Sam's, but then something knocks against my legs, pushing us apart.

I look down, and realize the thing—the animal—that pushed us apart is—

"Mackerel!" I say in shock, bending down as he wags his tail so hard his whole body is practically vibrating. He's trying to lick me, but he's moving too fast, and I start laughing. "What are you doing here, bud?"

That's when I realize: If there's a Mackerel, there must be an Aiden close by.

I get up slowly, and for the first time in six months, I see Aiden, standing a few feet away, holding Mack's leash.

Aiden is looking right at me.

And he doesn't look happy.

4

AIDEN

Emma's blue eyes are wide in disbelief, but I can't look away. Time has slowed, and the rest of the world seems to fade, so the only thing I can see is Emma. She looks the same—short blond hair, big blue eyes—but she's wearing a coat I've never seen before. And the expression on her face is one I've never seen before, either. She slowly stands up, and the rest of the world comes back into focus. Mackerel sits next to her, looking back and forth between us.

And then I see the guy standing just behind Emma. He takes a step forward and says, "Why, hello there," bending down to pet Mackerel.

But Mackerel just peers up at me, and Emma stares at me with the unfamiliar look on her face.

"Your dog is really cute," the guy says, petting Mackerel.

Mackerel licks his lips, then walks over to me.

Emma and I are still staring at each other, fat snowflakes gently falling to the ground. I haven't seen her in six months, and the last time I saw her I didn't know it'd be the last time I'd see her for so long, and now she's here, in person, and it should feel so good to see her, but it doesn't. It's like a car driving by, its windows down. I hear little bits of my favorite song, but then the car is gone. So is the music.

The expression on Emma's face is still unreadable, and I hate that I don't know what she's thinking or feeling.

The guy stands up and snaps his fingers. "That's the dog from the picture!"

Emma finally breaks eye contact with me, but she seems confused as she says, "What picture?"

The guy laughs. "The one on your phone?"

I put my hand on Mackerel's head, feeling protective of my dog, not liking that this guy, this stranger, knows anything about Mack at all. This boyfriend of Emma's.

Emma smiles, but it's forced. "That's right. This is Mackerel." She laughs apprehensively. "He shakes paws, if you want to introduce yourself."

Why is she talking about Mackerel like I'm not even standing right here?

"He probably won't do it with you." I can practically feel the acid in my voice. “He only does tricks for people he knows. Not strangers.”

Emma shoots me a surprised look.

“Well, let’s fix that,” the guy says, bending down again, talking to Mackerel in a sugary-sweet voice. “I’m Sam; it’s nice to meet you.”

“And he doesn’t respond to baby talk,” I add.

Emma shoots me another surprised look, but this guy, Sam, goes on with the baby talk. “Aren’t you just the handsomest dog there is?”

Mack looks up at me pleadingly. “We should go. I’m picking up food for my family.”

Sam pops back up. “Thanks for letting me pet your dog.”

But neither Emma nor I say anything.

Sam glances back and forth between us. “So . . . you’re the neighborhood friend?”

“What?” Emma and I both say at the same time.

“When you showed me the picture of the dog—”

“Mackerel,” Emma and I say at the same time, without looking at each other.

“Right, Mackerel,” Sam says. “You said he belonged to your neighborhood friend.”

“Neighborhood friend?” I echo.

Emma still won't meet my eye. "I think I said *childhood* friend?"

"What does *that* mean?" I ask with so much bitterness in my voice that even Sam seems uncomfortable.

"Aiden, it's true, we've known each other since childhood—"

"And that's it?" I interrupt.

Emma looks at me urgently. "Aiden. No, of course that's not—"

"Ah, Aiden!" Sam says. "I don't think Emma mentioned your name before."

I snort. "Sure sounds like she didn't."

"I should have known I'd run into you here." Emma is trying to smooth things over, like she always does. But some things can't be smoothed over. She puts her arms out like she's going to hug me, and I feel myself take a small step back, so she lets her arms fall.

"Why should you know you'd run into me? Like I'm just waiting around for you?"

Emma laughs awkwardly. "I mean, there are only so many places to eat in Briar Glen? And it's . . ." She trails off, waiting for me to fill in the blank, for me to talk about Cup o' Jo, but I'm not her puppet.

"Yeah, we don't have endless options like you do in New York City," I snap back.

I see the hurt in Emma's eyes and wish I could have a do-over on the last five minutes of my life, starting from when Mackerel saw Emma and bolted for her.

"Emms, remember that Korean taco place we went to last week?" Sam asks.

I glare at him. *Emms?*

He ignores my glare and says, "Anyway, it's nice to meet you, Aiden, no matter how long you've known Emma!" He sticks out a hand for a handshake.

Seriously?

I'm not Emma's puppet, and I'm not this guy's trained animal. I cross my arms, ignoring his gesture, and he slings an arm around Emma's shoulder like that's what he meant to do all along.

My hands are losing feeling. And I know it's not from the cold. Mack leans against me, like he's protecting me. From what, I'm not sure.

"The Korean tacos are amazing!" Emma goes on. "You'd really like them. I think I sent you a picture?"

"Maybe."

But I know what picture she's talking about. I'd been playing guitar, and my phone had dinged, and I'd been so excited to see her name pop up. But the message had just been a picture of a taco. Not an explanation, a joke, any indication that she'd even meant to send the photo to me. For all I knew it could have been an accident. Maybe even a picture she'd meant to send to someone else. Now I realize that someone else could have been Sam, and my hands lose what little feeling they had.

"Obviously, the food is not why I moved to New York," Emma hurries on. "Easton is incredible, and they teach math so differently. I think I told you already, but we're learning about the actual theories behind it all, and it's so cool!"

"Oh." I remember another text, from when she'd first started at Easton. A picture of her math homework, and she'd written that she wondered if she'd made a mistake by switching schools. She had made it sound like a joke, and I'd just written back something like "You can do it." Because she could, but she didn't need to hear that from me.

Sam slurps from a coffee cup now, and I realize it's a Java Junction one.

"Want a sip?" Sam says, offering his coffee to Emma.

"No, thanks," Emma says, not meeting my eyes again.

"I thought you hated coffee," I say. "And Java Junction."

They both look at me, and Emma laughs strangely. "Easton has a lot more homework than I'm used to. The classes are so much work! I needed caffeine to stay up late and I was getting tired of soda, so Sam gave me a peppermint mocha, and I've been hooked ever since."

"How nice" is all I think to say.

"I feel a little bad that she got so addicted to them," Sam says.

Emma grins at Sam.

They grin at each other, and she likes this guy, she really does.

"We should probably get back, shouldn't we?" Sam asks. "Don't want to keep your parents waiting too long, and this snow is getting cold." He brushes flakes off his jacket.

This stranger, with Emma's family, in her house. This stranger, at Cup o' Jo. Did Emma get a peppermint hot chocolate? Did she even think of me if she did? I feel heat rising in my face. But it's not anger. It's embarrassment. I'm embarrassed at how hard this is for me.

"Though, Aiden, if you're picking up food, we can wait for you and walk back together," Sam offers. "Since you live near Emma?"

"I can find my own way." The words come out choked. "I've lived in Briar Glen my whole life. It's not like I'm going to get lost." Though right now I feel more lost than I ever have in my life.

"Aiden," Emma tries again. There is pain in her eyes. But she has nothing to be hurt about.

Sam puts his arm around Emma again, still holding his

Java Junction cup, and everything is moving in slow motion. A nightmare.

Emma stares at me, but I tear my eyes away from her.

Her and her boyfriend.

I snap on Mackerel's leash and yank open the Cup o' Jo door. "I guess you got everything you wanted, didn't you, Emma?"

I walk into Cup o' Jo before she can say anything else to me.

APRIL, EIGHT YEARS AGO.

Emma carefully pulled her trifold poster out of her mom's trunk. "You sure you don't need help?" her mom asked.

Emma looked around at the chaotic school parking lot and said, "Nah, I'm fine."

"Okay, have a good day," her mom said, closing the trunk and getting back in the car.

Emma didn't have a free hand to wave, so she just shouted, "Bye!"

She walked slowly into the gym, where her third-grade classmates were in a line, waiting to go upstairs to their classroom.

She surveyed her classmates' social studies projects on United States cities. Most kids had single-sided posters, and some other kids had dioramas. Emma didn't see any other posters like hers. She joined her class's line, feeling proud of her project.

She accidentally knocked into Jason, who whipped his head

around to scowl at Emma. His expression changed to a smirk when he saw her poster board.

"Do not even tell me that is your project," he said, still smirking.

"It is!" Emma said, holding the board protectively. "I love New York City."

"Teacher's pet much?" he sneered.

"What does working hard on a project have to do with being a teacher's pet?" Emma asked, in genuine confusion.

Jason opened his mouth like he wanted to say something, but he let it close, and he turned back around again.

"What city did you pick?" Emma asked, undeterred.

"What?"

"For the social studies project!" Emma said. "Which city did you pick?"

"Miami," Jason said, bored.

"Where is it?" Emma asked, trying to stand on tiptoe to see if Jason had put his project on the floor.

"In Florida," he said sarcastically. Then, in a moment of kindness, at least for Jason, he reached into his backpack and pulled out a rumpled stack of notebook papers, stapled together in one corner, and showed it to Emma.

"Isn't it supposed to be on white paper?" she asked.

Jason scowled at her again and mumbled, “Whatever,” before turning back around.

The board was getting heavy in Emma’s hands, and she shifted.

A few minutes later, Aiden walked into the gym and saw Emma holding a huge poster board. He got into line behind her, and she smiled when she saw him.

“How did your project turn out?” Emma asked.

Aiden looked at his own flimsy poster board that he’d hastily filled in last night, his grandma grumbling about procrastination. “I think it’s okay.”

“Why did you pick Milwaukee, anyway?” Emma asked. “You’ve never even been there!”

“It’s got a cool name! I guess I was distracted, too: We’re going to foster a new dog this weekend!”

“Aiden, that’s amazing!” Emma said, jumping up and down.

She smacked Jason with the board, and he turned around. “Oooh, Aiden, that’s amazing,” he mocked in a cruel falsetto.

Aiden blushed, but Emma ignored Jason. “What kind of dog? What is its name?”

“It’s some kind of daschund-beagle-Chihuahua mix,” Aiden said, still feeling his blush.

“He must be so cute!”

Jason was ready to keep making fun of Emma, but his friend Graham showed up and Jason lost interest.

"His name is Mushington," Aiden went on, more eager to talk now that Jason wasn't paying attention. Aiden's family had started fostering dogs the year before. Secretly, Aiden was still hoping his family would end up adopting one of the dogs themselves, but it hadn't happened . . . yet.

"Please tell me I can meet him this weekend," Emma said.

"Yes, of course. How did your report turn out?" Aiden asked. He wanted to keep talking about Mushington, but he didn't want any further attention from Jason.

"I can't wait to present it! Did you know that there are over eight hundred languages spoken in New York City?"

"You told me," Aiden said, smiling. Emma's family had gone to the city over spring break a few weeks ago and Emma hadn't stopped talking about it. She'd told him she wanted to live there when she was a grown-up, but she'd also told him she'd wanted to live in Canada, Antarctica, and Italy.

"Pizza came from New York City, too! In the 1800s," Emma went on.

"You told me that, too," Aiden said, laughing now.

Emma wanted to tell him more, but it was time for the class to go upstairs to their room. Emma walked slowly with her big poster board, and Aiden shuffled along, clutching his messy poster board.

Social studies was the third class of the morning, the last one before lunch, and soon it was time for everyone to share their projects. The students presented in order of where they sat in the classroom, and Emma bounced in her seat in anticipation, patiently sitting through Delaney's explanation of her diorama about Washington, DC, then Max's presentation about Philadelphia.

Finally, Ms. Lynn said, "Emma, your turn."

Emma picked up her board and practically skipped to the front of the room, bumping into Jason's head on the way. "Ouch!" he said loudly, but no one seemed to hear him.

She placed the board on Ms. Lynn's desk. She looked at Aiden, who smiled at her encouragingly, then opened the board slowly.

She waited for gasps of approval, of amazement, but nothing. Resolute, she explained the different parts of her board. "New York City is made up of five boroughs," she said, pointing to the map she had drawn with colored pencils.

"Guess how many people live in New York City, in all those boroughs." Emma's eyes gleamed in excitement.

Aiden saw the bored looks on his classmates' faces. He felt his own face starting to flush.

"Emma, this isn't really a question-and-answer-type report," Ms. Lynn said. "Just tell me—"

"Over eight million!" Emma blurted out. "Can you believe that? Do you know how many people live in Kentucky?"

"Emma—" Ms. Lynn started again.

"Not even five million people!" Emma said. "If we do the math, that's a difference of more than three million people!"

"Oh, are we in a first-grade math class now?" chortled Jason.

"Jason!" Ms. Lynn snapped. "You just lost five minutes of recess."

Emma kept going, though. "This is the Statue of Liberty. I drew it," she said, pointing, and then whirling around to face her class, most of whom were barely paying attention.

"It was a gift from France. That's where it was made, and then taken apart again so it could be put on a boat to cross the ocean, and then it was reassembled in New York! So much work," she said, mostly to herself.

As she talked, Aiden looked around the room and felt his face get even warmer. Some kids were doodling in their notebooks now; others were yawning. Jason glared at Emma, his arms crossed.

"New York City is such a cool city," Emma continued. "My family and I went there over spring break. Someday I want to live there and—"

"Emma, try to stick with facts, not anecdotes," Ms. Lynn said.

"New York City is such a cool city," Jason mimicked in a toddler voice. Then, in his normal voice: "If you love New York City so much, maybe you should just leave Briar Glen and move there. You'll fit right in with all the other weirdos."

"Jason!" Ms. Lynn cried. "You come outside with me in the hallway when Emma is done!"

Emma looked at Jason, momentarily speechless, then continued: "There are almost eight hundred bridges and tunnels in all of New York City. The Brooklyn Battery Tunnel is the longest underwater tunnel for cars in North America, and the second longest is the Holland Tunnel. The Manhattan Bridge and Williamsburg Bridge connect Brooklyn to Manhattan, and they're so big that a subway even runs over them. The Brooklyn Bridge also connects Brooklyn to Manhattan, but it only allows for people walking across or biking across it. It was the first bridge with steel cable wires—"

"And your time is up," Ms. Lynn said. "Anyone have any questions for Emma about New York City?"

"But I'm not done with my presentation yet," Emma said.

"Sorry, Emma, everyone gets three minutes," Ms. Lynn said. "I know you want to hear everyone else's reports."

"I do," Emma said, but she didn't move.

"Take your seat," Ms. Lynn said, the patience beginning to evaporate from her voice.

Emma shook her head. "It's not fair, though! Jason interrupted me twice, and that took time away from my report."

Aiden wished Emma would just sit down. He had a bad feeling about where this conversation was heading.

"And I'm talking to him in the hallway in just a second," Ms. Lynn said.

Aiden watched Jason wave at Emma.

Emma shook her head again. "It's not fair that I lose presentation time because Jason was rude."

"It's not fair, it's not fair," Jason mimicked again, in another baby voice, then muttered, "weirdo."

Emma glared at Jason. She took deep breaths. She told herself not to cry. Not to yell.

"That's it, out in the hallway, immediately!" Ms. Lynn said.

The class *ooh*ed—if you went in the hallway, you were in really big trouble—but Jason took his time getting up from his desk, while Emma continued to glare at him. Just before he stepped into the hall, he turned and gave Emma another wave.

Emma breathed deeply, looking out into the hallway, while the TA, Ms. Miranda, tried to shush everyone as she took over the class. She gently suggested that Emma sit down, but Emma shook her head and stayed next to her project. She tore her eyes away from the hallway—she couldn't even see Jason or Ms. Lynn, anyway—and looked at Aiden.

To Aiden's surprise, Emma smiled at him. He couldn't believe how calm she was.

A scowling Jason came back into the classroom a few minutes later, along with Ms. Lynn. He trudged over to Emma and robotically said, "I'm sorry, Emma."

Emma smiled sweetly. "I'll send you a postcard when I move to New York."

Ms. Lynn sighed. "Emma . . ."

"Can I finish my report now?"

The teacher checked the clock and sighed again. "After lunch."

"Thank you!"

The third-grade class lined up, and Emma got in line right behind Aiden.

"You okay?" Aiden asked.

"Never better," Emma said, but her smile was tight. "Maybe we don't have to talk about it now?"

Aiden nodded. "Did you know that Mushington has really short legs?"

Emma was confused for a second. "The dog you're going to foster?"

"He also hates carrots."

"Carrots? Like eating them? Or, like, looking at them?"

Aiden shrugged. "The shelter just wrote *hates carrots.*"

"Why would a dog hate carrots?"

"I guess I'll find out in a few days?"

"How?" Emma wrinkled her nose.

"I'll ask him?"

They looked at each other and laughed.

5

EMMA

Aiden and Mackerel go into Cup o' Jo. My face stings with shock, with hurt. I knew coming to Briar Glen would mean seeing Aiden again. I'd known it on a fact-based level. Aiden lives in Briar Glen, therefore I'd see him. But that was mostly as far as I'd let my mind go. Mostly. I knew I should have texted him, told him I was coming. I should have told him a lot of things. And I tried, at first.

On my first train ride to New York, six months ago, I started so many texts to Aiden telling him I was sorry for leaving Briar Glen so abruptly. I told him that my feelings were hurt that he wasn't supportive of my decision to go to Easton. I told him how important he was to me, how much I cared about him. I told him just because I didn't live in Briar Glen anymore didn't mean we couldn't be friends.

Friends.

My fingers got stuck on the word, because it sounded hollow. And because it wasn't true. Not entirely. He *was* my friend. But he was also my . . . Aiden. He was the person who knew me better than anyone else on the planet, the person I felt most comfortable with, the person I could say anything to. Well, almost anything. I couldn't say, then, that I'd been starting to think about him . . . differently. That seeing him and spending time with him didn't feel like something I wanted to do, but something I *needed* to do. That being close to him, almost touching him, was something I craved. That the way he smiled at me, the way he looked at me, made feel like the most special person in the world.

I couldn't say any of this to him, because I could barely admit these things to myself.

I told myself that once I got settled in the city Aiden and I would pick up where we had left off. The problem was, I wasn't sure *where* we had left off. Worse, I didn't know how to find it.

Finally, after I'd been in the city for a few days, I texted him a picture of Rockefeller Center, saying "Hi from NYC!"

He'd sent back a waving hand emoji and then a picture of Mackerel in the sun, and we'd never talked about my sudden departure.

Still, everything reminded me of Aiden. Someone on my dorm

floor played guitar, and the song she played most was Green Day's "Last Night on Earth," which was one of the last songs Aiden learned how to play on his guitar before I left.

There were so many dogs in the city, so many more than I would have expected or had remembered from previous vacations, but a lot of them wore coats or little sweaters, something I knew Mackerel would scoff at.

There was a diner across the street from Easton, but everything cost three times what it cost at Cup o' Jo, and the food was half as good.

I drafted so many messages to Aiden, telling him all these silly little things, but ended up sending only a handful of them. Because I realized that's what they were—silly little things.

His responses to messages I did end up sending weren't unfriendly, but they weren't . . . Aiden. He added little thumbs-ups to pictures, wrote back things like "Looks cool." He mostly sent me pictures of Mackerel. When I'd ask him how things were, how he was, the answer was always "Fine." So soon I started answering his questions the same way. School was fine. New York City was fine. Everything was fine. And somehow, I never got a chance to tell him about Sam.

I guess you got everything you wanted, didn't you, Emma? The words bounce around in my head painfully.

I want Aiden and Mackerel to come back out of Cup o' Jo, to do the reunion all over again. But I don't even know what I'd say.

I try to think what to say to Sam, how to explain what just happened with Aiden, but he takes another sip of his drink and says, "Ready? I feel kinda bad that we didn't eat at your parents' house."

"My house," I say automatically.

"You know what I meant."

Do I?

We walk in the cold night air, the snow just flurries now. The tree twinkles behind the gazebo, and some bundled-up families are taking pictures in front of it.

Sam and I are quiet until he says, "Was Aiden one of your good friends?"

It's surreal to hear Sam say Aiden's name. His name feels like something I need to hold on to gently. It's even worse to hear him referred to in the past tense.

"We just had a falling-out," I say maybe a little too ominously. It's the same thing I've told Sam every time he's asked about my friends in Briar Glen before I would change the subject.

Sam reaches out and grabs my hand. "I'm sorry for all the questions." We stop walking, and he looks into my eyes. "Are you okay?"

"I'm all right," I say. "It's just a little . . . weird to be here after so long." But I don't know if *weird* is a big enough word for everything I'm feeling.

"Remember, I want to understand."

I think about our conversation on the train, about his summer camp, try to picture cute little Sam at a cute little summer camp, and nod.

"I just mean I can understand how disorienting this must feel. I guess I never really had a sense of *home* in one particular building. More just like the city itself. We moved apartments a few times when I was a kid. The apartment my parents live in now isn't where I grew up. We had a huge brownstone on the Upper West Side when I was little, but my parents had it renovated, and we lived in a building a few blocks over. And then, when I started at Easton, my parents ended up selling the brownstone, anyway, and moving to the apartment they have now."

"Why haven't you told me that before?" I ask, wondering what else he hasn't told me. Then I think about things I haven't told him.

"It was a long time ago. I'm over it now. But I guess I can understand what it's like to go home and not really be at home, you know?"

We've reached my street, and I see my house, glowing. For as long as I've been away, this house will always be my home. I want to tell Sam that, but the thought feels like another one of those things I want to hold on to gently, so I don't say anything.

I stop for a second and take it all in. My home. Sam wraps his arms around me. We gaze at my house together, and his closeness, his touch, brings me back to the present moment. *My boyfriend is at my house*, I remind myself.

"Those Santa and reindeer decorations used to be my mom's when she was a kid," I say.

"That's sweet you still put them out."

"Sweet?" I echo.

"Yeah, look at them." He pulls away from me and points to the cracks in one of the reindeer's hooves.

"Yeah?" I ask, confused.

"No offense, but you guys could have replaced those and upgraded to something fancier along the way?"

"But it's not just the decorations. It's about my family, about my home, about my memories. My origin story. We're kinda attached to the Christmas decorations."

"Yes, of course," he says quickly, looking at me that way that usually makes me feel all gooey inside. But then he says, "I guess I can't imagine being so attached to Christmas decorations."

"Jeez, when you put it that way," I joke. *Am* I joking, though?

He laughs, then is quiet for a minute before saying, "But seriously. We've been outside a lot today. Can we get inside where it's warmer?"

I want to show him the candy cane decorations lining our path, tell him about the pretend sword fights Kerry and I used to have with them, but he's already walking up the porch steps.

When we get inside, it still smells like freshly baked cookies.

My parents and my sister are all sat on the couch. They've got *A Christmas Story* on the TV, but my mom and sister are reading, and my dad is tapping away on his laptop, and no one is really watching the movie.

"Hi!" I say and am met with a "Hi!" from my parents and a grunt from Kerry.

I slide my boots off, and Sam takes his off, too.

"How was Cup o' Jo?" my mom asks.

I think about the way Aiden looked at me, like I was a stranger, how hard it was to talk to him. *Everything I wanted.* "It was fine." And then, a second later, "I saw Aiden, too. And Mackerel." I smile just a tiny bit, thinking of Mack's lopsided ears.

My mom puts down her book and her reading glasses. "I forgot to tell you: Your dad and I ran into Aiden and Mack tonight! I told Aiden you must have so much to catch up on."

"And probably Mackerel, too," my dad jokes.

I feel everyone in the room looking at me. Including Sam. "I don't even know where I'd start," I say truthfully. Then, before my mom can ask me more questions about Aiden, I add, "It smells so good in here!"

"Help yourself to dessert," my dad says. "Some of it is for the holiday party, but we certainly have enough to spare."

"And if you're still hungry, there's macaroni and cheese," my mom chimes in.

I wish Sam and I had just stayed home for dinner and not gone to Cup o' Jo. I wish almost every part of the last hour could have gone differently. But I've been so distracted tonight I forgot that my parents had mentioned the party earlier. "You're still doing the holiday party?" I ask, looking around the house.

"Why wouldn't we?" my mom asks. "All the neighborhood families take turns, and this is our year!"

I gesture at the cluttered coffee table, covered with magazines, books, crumbs, and the winter snow globe that plays music. The jumbled mess feels a bit like my brain at the moment.

"You think the house will be ready in time?" I ask.

Will my heart be ready in time?

Kerry says, "Since when do you care what the house looks like? We all know your room is organized to perfection, but you've never really cared about the rest of the place."

I'm conscious of Sam, who is standing behind me in the entryway. "It's just interesting to see everything from a different point of view."

Kerry rolls her eyes. "Yes, because you've traveled around the world and have returned to our humble abode."

For once I'm grateful for my sister's sarcasm, and I stick out my tongue at her. We both laugh, and Sam waits for a few seconds, but then he joins the laughter, too.

"I think I need dessert," I say.

In the kitchen, I dig through the fridge, open storage containers, pull foil off plates, and assemble a little plate of chocolate chip brownies—one of my favorite things my parents bake—a star-shaped sugar cookie, and chocolate shortbread cookies.

I bring the plate into the living room, shove some of the magazines out of the way, and place my collection of desserts in the empty space. My parents and sister are taking up the couch, so I move a snowman blanket off the loveseat, and Sam and I sit. I offer the plate to Sam, but he shakes his head.

I munch away on my dessert, suddenly very aware of how loudly I'm chewing. I think about Sam's parents' pristine apartment. I'm not sure if they even owned a TV.

My mom puts down her book and says, "So, Sam, what's your favorite pizza place? Bagel place?"

Sam says, almost like he's not even thinking about it, "Joe's Pizza and Zabar's."

"Have we gone to those places before?" my mom asks my dad. "I can't remember."

My dad says, "Zabar's sounds right. I think that's where we got black-and-white cookies. Wasn't it?"

"No, the black-and-white cookies were from—"

"Guys!" I say. "You're making New York sound like some kind of mysterious, faraway land. You've been there. You know what it's like."

Kerry says, "Yeah, we're not total country bumpkins. Did everyone forget that I live in Boston?"

"Oh, you live in Boston?" I say, smirking at her.

"Hilarious," Kerry deadpans.

"Well, on to non–New York things," my dad starts. "Sam, how long have you and your family been—"

"Last question!" I interrupt. Then I say, more calmly, "It's been a long day."

Sam says agreeably, "It's fine."

My dad carries on: "How long has your family been skiing and snowboarding?"

"As long as I can remember," Sam says. "I don't even know when I learned how to snowboard! Maybe when I was three or four?"

"See, he's known how to snowboard forever," I say, turning to my dad. "Now can we watch the movie? Please?" I add, in a kinder tone.

"Okay, okay." My dad chuckles. "But don't think I've forgotten about those baby photo albums, either!"

"Dad," I groan. "Sam doesn't want to see those."

"Oh yes I do," Sam says, leaning into me..

"Shush!" Kerry says.

"Seriously? How many times have you seen this movie?" I ask.

"One less now, unless you stop talking!" she teases.

And then I remember: It's the holidays, and my boyfriend is at my house. I cuddle up with Sam and let my head rest against his shoulder. *Everything is okay. Better than okay.*

But when I crawl into bed a few hours later, my mind is a tangled mess. I feel like I need a pause button. I think about Sam in my house, in my living room, sitting with me on the loveseat, showing him my childhood bedroom. My origin story. I snuggle happily into my blankets. He's here. In the house where I'd learned how to walk; the house where I'd fought with Kerry and made up with Kerry; the house where I'd played Barbie for hours on end.

And also the house where I'd spent countless hours with Aiden. We'd built blanket forts, played endless games of hide-and-seek, and just hung out. I realize the loveseat I sat on with Sam I'd also sat on with Aiden. The same space that was new to Sam was so familiar to Aiden. I was used to seeing Aiden in my house, and now someone else was seeing it for the first time. But Sam isn't aware of all the ghosts, of all the memories I've created here.

I think about the way Aiden looked at me, the coldness to his voice, like he was talking to a stranger. I guess I am. I toss my blanket off. Kerry snores next to me on the trundle bed. *Lucky*, I think.

I open my beside drawer, even though I'm not sure what I'm looking for. There are some lip balms, earring backs, and bookmarks. But, underneath it all, I see the words: *Emma and Aiden are the bestest friends ever.* It's scrawled in glitter pen by eight-year-old me. I close the drawer.

This house and its ghosts.

When I go downstairs for breakfast the next morning, Sam is already at the dining room table, a bowl of cereal in front of him, talking to my dad.

"Morning, sunshine!" my dad says.

"Morning," I say back, but it's Sam I'm looking at. He's picked me up for morning classes and saw me in pajamas on a day I overslept, but I feel self-conscious. I tug the zipper on my hoodie up a little bit higher.

Sam is dressed in jeans and a long-sleeved collared shirt and asks, "Want to go to the Briar Glen holiday market after breakfast? I know we didn't make a plan for when to go, but I was thinking today was a good day."

I stare at him blankly, my mind not registering that he's asking me something about Briar Glen. But then I nod. "Sure, sounds good. Sorry, I guess I'm still tired!"

My boyfriend at the Briar Glen holiday market.

Sam says, "Maybe you need some coffee?"

"That'll stunt your growth!" my dad says with a chuckle.

Sam says guiltily, "Whoops! Emma has been drinking coffee at Easton. I kind of got her hooked on peppermint mochas."

"You don't have to tattle on me," I tease. "I think I'm over twelve." Sam making plans to go to a holiday market I've been going to since I was little; now he's telling my dad I drink coffee? It's all making me feel fidgety, irritable. "I think I should get dressed. For the market." I'm still processing my blooming grumpiness, and it hits me: Aiden will be at the holiday market, with his family at their woodworking booth.

The prospect overwhelms me.

Kerry wanders in, munching on a bagel, already dressed as well, and my mom trails behind her, yawning, wrapping her robe around herself.

"I guess we're not getting any worms today, are we?" my mom asks.

"Guess not." I laugh. It's something she's said to me almost every weekend of my life, and I'm grateful for the familiarity of the phrase. *But maybe not all familiar things are good*, I think as I get dressed and ready. *Sam*, I think instead. *Sam at the Briar Glen holiday market.*

Sam and *Aiden at the Briar Glen holiday market.*

There's no more time to think, though, because my parents are calling for me, and soon my mom, dad, and Sam and I are all out the door. Kerry stays home because she says she wants to get a jumpstart on party prep, but we all know it's so she can have an actual private conversation with her girlfriend, Kristy.

"It's time for you and me to talk more," my dad says once we're outside, putting a hand on Sam's shoulder, guiding Sam away from me.

"It is?" I ask, feeling panic spreading in my stomach.

"It is," my dad says, walking with Sam. "Plus, the roasted chestnuts at the market are incredible, and they almost always sell out. Let's go ahead?"

"Please don't tell Sam anything embarrassing!" I call.

"I won't tell him anything *too* embarrassing," my dad calls back.

I sigh, halfway between embarrassment and humor. And more than halfway confused about seeing Aiden again.

My mom puts her arm around me. "You know your dad has been looking forward to meeting Sam since the second we heard about him."

"What are they even talking about?" I ask, watching their retreating figures.

My mom chuckles. "Knowing your father, it could be the weather, something that happened to him when he was a kid, or a fun fact he learned yesterday."

"Or something from my childhood."

"Or something from your childhood," my mom says, chuckling again. My childhood, which is filled with memories of Aiden.

We walk in silence for a few minutes. It's overcast, and the air has the smell of impending snow. I didn't realize how much I had missed the smell until now.

I look again at my dad and Sam. My *boyfriend*. "Sam's great, isn't he?" I think about his puppy-dog eyes, the way my body tingles when he touches me. I feel a grin sneaking onto my face.

"He's lovely," my mom agrees.

"Lovely," I repeat. "We haven't said that word yet. Love."

"That's okay. You just met him. You guys are still getting to know each other."

"We've been dating for five months."

"I know that seems like a long time, but think about a five-month-old baby, how much they still have to learn."

"You're comparing my relationship to a baby?"

"No, sorry, that came out wrong," she says. "Your relationship is still in its infancy, is all."

"And?" I prod.

"You're still learning about each other. It takes time to love someone."

"What about love at first sight? Isn't that what happened with you and Dad?"

"It was." My mom looks wistful. "But we still didn't say it to each other for a few months."

"Ew, let's not talk about it." I'm starting to feel squirmy and grossed out.

She laughs. "You and Aiden have known each other for so long, and know so much about each other."

My smile fades at the mention of Aiden's name, and my legs suddenly feel rubbery. Just when I thought I'd put him out of my mind. "What does he have to do with anything?" I ask in a tone I don't recognize.

"It's nothing," my mom says, waving her hand. "I don't know. Maybe I've been watching too many holiday movies. But I've always thought you and Aiden would end up together someday. It's a parent thing."

"Aiden?" My voice is shrill. Has she been inside my head, inside my heart? Has she known about my feelings for him? Has anyone else? Then again, I barely know about *my* feelings for Aiden. All I know is they don't make sense.

"It's just one of those mom things," she says vaguely. "I know how happy you and Aiden make each other. How easy it is with you two. How well you understand each other."

Despite myself, I feel another grin forming. But this smile feels different than when I was talking about Sam. That smile felt new. This smile feels like it's been there forever. Like Aiden. He felt like an extension of me. The way he could sometimes figure out what I was feeling before I could figure it out myself. The way he listened to whatever ideas popped into my head. The way he played guitar. His low voice, singing when he thought no one was listening.

I shake my head, snap myself out of it. "Sam is easygoing, too! And sensible, and smart, and driven. He's already thinking about where he wants to apply for medical school."

We're just passing the record store, which means we're getting close to the holiday market. And sure enough, I can smell the roasting chestnuts.

My mom says lightly, "Did he forget that you guys are seventeen?"

"Mom," I say impatiently. "He's planning for his future. He likes to plan things." I don't say that this is one of the things that separates him from Aiden.

"That's great! And he makes you happy? He listens to what you have to say?"

I think about the way Sam looks at me, the way he showed me around the city. How much he likes to talk about his career path, how he's trying to help me figure out what kind of job I might want someday.

"Of course he does." I hear the hesitation in my voice.

My mom studies me for a moment. "I just want you to be happy. That's all anyone wants for their kids. Happiness."

I'm aching to ask her more about what she was talking about when she brought up Aiden, but we're at the town square, and the market is in full swing. We walk past all kinds of booths: Vendors are selling freshly constructed wreaths from a local tree farm, there's fudge made with local maple syrup, hats knitted using local sheep's wool. Bundled-up shoppers bustle all around us. My dad and Sam are in the line for roasted chestnuts, but my mom and I head in the opposite direction. A direction, I realize, closer to Aiden.

I see kids from my high school, faces I haven't seen in half a year. Sky, a girl I played with in second grade, waves at me, and I know I should talk to her, but I'm starting to feel overwhelmed. Aiden's family's booth is always toward the back of the market. I'm getting closer and closer to him.

My mom stops at a booth selling handblown glass ornaments, but I keep walking, my legs feeling rubbery again.

Then, I see Aiden.

I watch him, smiling as he holds up a handcrafted sled while he talks with a customer. How can I miss someone who is standing a few feet away from me? I feel even more overwhelmed now. And something else, some sort of dull pain in my chest.

I watch his hands as he rings up another customer. He isn't wearing the gloves I gave him.

I think about the conversation I just had with my mom. Of course Sam makes me happy. He's a good guy. Of course he listens to me. My mom was right: She's been watching too many holiday movies. Aiden and I are just friends. *Were* friends. No, I couldn't think about Aiden in the past tense when Sam brought him up last night, and I can't think about Aiden in the past tense now.

Maybe there is a way to fix things with Aiden. Though I'm not sure what those things are, or how to fix them.

I feel that dull pain again.

6

AIDEN

"This will go superfast!" I say, handing a sled to a little girl who is standing with her parents.

"Oooh, it'll be perfect for the sled race!" the little girl says.

One of the moms chuckles. "As long as you wear your helmet."

"Mom," the little girl groans.

"Have fun," I tell her. "You're braver than me!"

"Are you too scared to do the race?"

"Jade!" her mom says.

"No, it's okay. She's not wrong."

"And you sell sleds?" Jade asks in confusion.

"Maybe it'll help me overcome my fear. One day."

The moms laugh and turn to walk away, Jade clutching her sled.

They leave, and then when I turn around, Emma is at the

other end of the tent. Even though I just saw her last night, her presence still shocks me. I haven't gotten used to Briar Glen without her. It'd be like getting used to a night sky without stars. But I've become used to the ache her absence has created.

She smiles at me, but it's almost like she feels shy, which isn't a feeling I've ever known Emma to have. Around anyone.

I remember my words to her last night, my coldness to her, and also the heat from my embarrassment at how painful it was to see her.

"Aiden! Your grandpa has made so much!" Emma spins around the tent in a slow circle, admiring the sleds, the sled ornaments, bookshelves, cheese boards, picture frames, pretty much anything and everything that can be crafted from wood. "This is amazing!" she says softly, without meeting my eye.

I start to say something less than kind, about how of course he's made a lot because she's been gone for a long time. But I look around, and it really is amazing how much he's made, the scope of his talent, and despite myself, I am proud of him. And the way Emma is avoiding my eye, I can't be cruel.

"Thanks," I finally say. "I'll tell him."

She looks up at me, and we stand there, gazing at each other, in an awkwardness I've never experienced with her. Well, at least not since last night.

"I'm sorry I haven't been in touch more." It's the first time I've admitted to anyone, even myself, how little we've spoken since June. "And I'm sorry for what I said last night, too. About getting everything you wanted," I add quickly. I want to elaborate, want to say how her boyfriend seems nice, but the words are stuck somewhere in my chest. *Her boyfriend.*

"It's okay. And no, I'm sorry. I tried to . . ."

I wait, but she doesn't say anything else.

Mackerel chooses this moment to crawl out of his dog bed in the corner of the tent. He stretches and trots over to Emma, tongue out, a doggy grin on his face.

Emma laughs, bends down. "I've missed you," she says. She doesn't look up when she says it.

"I've—I mean Mack—has missed you, too."

She rubs behind his ear, tugs gently on the one that always sticks up.

"You wouldn't believe the ridiculous outfits people in New York put their dogs in," she says, rubbing his belly. "Still, you'd be adorable in a sweater!"

She's trying, so hard, but I don't know if I have it in me to engage. I do feel myself smiling a bit, though, thinking about Mack in a hand-knit sweater.

Emma is smiling, too, and I wonder if she's picturing Mack in a silly sweater as well. Or if she's thinking about something else. Or someone else.

"There have been so many other things I've wanted to tell you about," she says, standing up. Mack looks disappointed, and sits on Emma's foot. "There is a girl on my floor who plays guitar, and she even plays 'Last Night on Earth.'"

I feel myself flinch just the tiniest bit at the mention of that song.

"And like I said, the food! You'd love the pizza!"

"Because we don't have pizza in these parts."

Emma is hurt, and it pains me.

"I'm joking," I say, even though I'm not sure if I am.

"Right. But the pizza *might* be better than Luigi's . . ." The Briar Glen pizzeria.

"Those *might* be fighting words." But I'm still not sure if I'm joking or not.

It's like she doesn't hear me. Maybe she doesn't because she just keeps talking, trying to fill the silence. "Did you know that New York City has over six thousand pizzerias?"

"Can't say that I did."

And still, there's more. "That means that we'd . . . I mean, you and me . . . I mean, *someone* would have to eat at sixteen different pizza places every single day for a year to visit them all."

Who is this *we*? Does she mean herself and her boyfriend? Herself and me?

"That's a lot of pizza." Then a memory comes crashing into my head. Or a series of memories. Emma and me eating pizza together at lunch every Friday in elementary school. Emma and me eating slices together at my house, her house. Sometimes with a movie on, sometimes with music. Sometimes no noise but the sound of our voices.

"The city is so beautiful in the fall," Emma continues, and I'm forced back into the present. "And there are holiday markets at all the parks."

"And where do you think you're standing now?" I'm trying to be funny, but it's still not enough to cut the tension, and I miss the easy, close past with Emma.

"I know! It's just . . . different."

Different is an understatement.

Mack is looking back and forth between Emma and me, until suddenly he springs up and barks, which is something he does maybe twice a year. Emma turns, just as I see Sam and her parents approaching.

Emma's parents are with her boyfriend. It's such an odd sentence to have in my head, and I feel the heat from the pain in my chest again.

They're all holding bags of roasted chestnuts, but the closer Emma's parents and Sam get, the louder Mack barks.

Mr. Sherman says loudly, "I guess besides last night we haven't seen you in a while!" He bends down, attempting to pet Mack, but Mack keeps barking.

He looks at Sam as he barks.

Sam tries to pet Mack, which makes him bark even louder.

"It's because he doesn't know you yet! I don't think he remembers you from last night!" Emma says over the barking, resting her gloved hand on Sam's arm. The motion makes something flip over in my stomach.

Sam puts out his hand for Mack to sniff, but Mack wants nothing to do with him. It's childish, but I wish I could give my dog a high five.

"It's so nice to see you again!" Mrs. Sherman says to me.

At all the noise Mack is making, Grandpa finishes up a birdhouse sale and walks over, frowning. "What's with him?"

Emma looks at me helplessly and I tell Mack to be quiet. He listens, which I'm both ungrateful and grateful for.

Grandpa starts talking to Emma's parents. Sam meets

Grandpa, which feels all wrong, and everyone says what a shame it is they haven't seen each other and they're looking forward to catching up. Sam stands next to Emma and hands her a hot chestnut. I look away.

"Can I give one to your dog?" Sam asks, holding up a chestnut.

"No, thanks, he's not supposed to eat chestnuts," I say between gritted teeth.

"Yes, it's the salt," Sam says. "Too much salt is bad for dogs. Sorry, that's something I should remember!"

Emma says, "Why? You don't have any pets."

"Grapes, raisins, gum, chocolate, onions, and garlic," Sam goes on. "Oh, I wanted to be a vet for a while when I was in middle school, so I started learning about household pets. Cats are allergic to the same things, plus a bunch of different plants. But I can't remember all of them."

"You wanted to be a vet?" Emma asks, looking at Sam curiously.

"Kind of weird, right, since I'm not really an animal guy?"

He snorts, like it's a joke, but Grandpa breaks away from his conversation with Emma's parents. "Never trust a man who says he's not an animal guy, Emma!"

Mr. Sherman pets Mack's head. "How can you not like animals?"

"I didn't say I don't like animals!" Sam squirms a bit. "I just didn't have any pets growing up."

"Why?" I ask.

Mr. and Mrs. Sherman and Grandpa and Emma all face Sam now. He squirms more, and I can't help but feel a twinge of joy at how uncomfortable he is.

"They're messy," Sam says, then looks at me. "No offense."

"None taken?" I say.

"You don't have a pet, either," Sam says, looking at Mr. and Mrs. Sherman.

Mrs. Sherman pets Mack's head now, too. "Mackerel turns up at our door so much he feels like our dog." She chuckles. "Plus, I'm allergic, apparently, though Mack's fur has never bothered me."

Emma looks at Mack lovingly, and Mack, thrilled at all the attention, starts wagging his tail.

"Not an animal guy," Grandpa mutters, shaking his head, then returns to his conversation with Emma's parents.

Sam looks nervously around the tent and whistles. "Your grandfather made all of this?"

"Yep."

Sam picks up a sled ornament and examines it. "Wow. I feel like I'm getting a splinter!"

Emma takes the ornament from his hand and says, "Should we get one for your parents?"

Any pleasure I felt before at Sam's expense disappears.

"That's a great idea, Emms," he says, draping an arm over her shoulders.

I feel the searing-hot pain in my chest again. Grandpa is still deep in conversation with Emma's parents. "I'll ring you up," I say, walking to the register.

"I didn't realize you worked here," Sam says.

Emma says, "He's been helping his grandpa since he was little." I think I hear pride in her voice. It doesn't take away the heat in my chest, though.

"Well, better you than me," Sam says, digging into his pocket for his credit card. "This seems like splinter city."

I glare at him, and Emma gives him a perplexed glance. Sam taps his card, then sees the stack of fliers next to our register. He picks one up and reads out loud, "'Briar Glen's forty-fourth annual winter festival.' It's only a few days from now. I'll still be here!"

"I told you about it on the train, remember?" Emma says. "It's a lot of fun. Well, except for the time—"

"We don't need to talk about that," I say, not wanting to relive my sledding injury.

Sam looks between Emma and me curiously.

"Anyway, pretty much all of Briar Glen goes," Emma says. She smiles nostalgically. I think about all the winter festivals we went to together, even *that* one.

"Who competes in the sledding race?" Sam asks.

"Whoever wants to," Emma says.

"What about Briar Glen visitors?"

"I don't know," Emma says. "I've never seen any tourists in it, I don't think."

"Oh, a tourist, am I?" Sam says teasingly, batting his eyelashes at Emma, and I have to look away again.

"It's not really a competition," I say, dusting off our cutting boards, anything to avoid looking at them.

But Sam doesn't seem to have heard me. "I totally have to do this! With all the snowboarding I've done, I'll definitely win."

"Not a competition!" I say again.

"Maybe I could use one of these sleds?"

I almost drop the cutting board I'm dusting.

Emma quickly says, "You can borrow one of ours."

"Are your sleds from here? Like, they're handmade?"

Grandpa made sleds for Emma, Kerry, and their parents, and the thought of Sam riding something Grandpa made, in my town's winter festival, makes my stomach churn.

"We can talk about it later," Emma says.

I wonder what it is she's so afraid to say in front of me.

Her parents and Grandpa walk over, just as Mrs. Sherman says to Grandpa, "We'll see you at our house tomorrow night, right?"

"What?" Emma and I say at the same time, both turning toward her.

"Our holiday party," Emma's mom says slowly.

"Right. At our house," Emma says. "Our house." Her eyes dart over to Sam. *What is that look she's giving him?*

Sam grins, and she grins back, and it's like this secret language that only they speak.

A customer has walked into the tent. They pick up a cutting board in the shape of a Christmas tree.

Sam says, "Looking forward to getting to know you more, Aiden. We'll see you tomorrow?"

We?

And he's talking about Emma's house, a place that is as comfortable to me as my own house.

Was, I remind myself. *Was.*

I watch Emma for just a second, and her eyes are huge, and I can tell she wants to say something, but I don't give her the chance. "Yep. We'll see you tomorrow!" I say to Sam. "Excuse me, though, I need to help this customer."

I walk away, Mack giving one final yip at Sam before following me.

DECEMBER, FOUR YEARS AGO.

Aiden looked around Cup o' Jo, thinking how different it seemed. Most of the tables had been pushed to the side, and there was a long table toward one of the corners of the café overflowing with all kinds of desserts. Cup o' Jo bustled with guests, everyone holding snowflake napkins, laughing and talking. Even though Jo hosted the party, people still brought their favorite desserts, and all the proceeds from the party went to the local animal shelter.

From the hallway at the back of the café, near the restrooms, came the faint sound of dogs barking. It was the foster dogs, in a penned-off area. All three were up for adoption, and there was one more—Aiden's family's next foster dog—on its way from the shelter.

Aiden saw Emma in a corner, near the bookshelves, balancing a mug of hot chocolate and a small plate.

Aiden waved, and Emma tried to wave back, but her hands were too full.

Emma made her way over to him, saying, "Excuse me," and, "Pardon me." The candy cane in her drink wobbled as she set her mug and plate down on a table. Then she put her hand over the top of her head, then up to Aiden's head, measuring their height.

"I think I've finally caught up with you! Well, as long as I'm wearing my boots," she said, peering down at her feet.

"I might grow more," Aiden said. "Do you see how tall my family is?" Mr. Cooper-Gallo stood next to his wife, near the dogs in the back, and Aiden and Emma both laughed. "Okay, so my family isn't known for their height."

Aiden turned back to Emma, and she was right, she'd grown, and she suddenly seemed much closer to him. His eyes were closer to hers.

"Your eyes look different," Emma said.

She said it like she was observing a scientific fact, but she didn't tell him how much she liked the golden flecks in his hazel eyes.

Aiden studied Emma's sparkling blue eyes. "Yours, too," he said, wanting to tell Emma that her eyes reminded him of an ocean. It seemed like an odd thing to say, especially since he hadn't actually seen an ocean in person since he was a little kid, so he bit his lip.

Emma broke the eye contact. "Chocolate chip brownie?" she

asked, nudging the gooey mound of chocolate on his plate. “The ones my parents brought?”

“Of course.” Aiden picked up the other brownie, flecked with red and white bits. “And peppermint. Made by Grandma.” He took a huge bite.

Emma laughed, touched his cheek, which bulged with food like a chipmunk’s. The touch made him stop chewing. Emma was surprised by how soft his skin was, and pulled her hand away.

Aiden could still feel the touch of Emma’s hand. Emma and Aiden had wrestled when they were kids, and they bumped into each other all the time, but Emma had never touched Aiden’s face before. It felt new.

Emma looked at her hand, which had just been on her best friend’s cheek. Why did she feel so strange?

Aiden chewed quickly and swallowed, searching for something to say. “It’s really the best time of year, isn’t? All the food.”

Emma nodded, distracted. “Did you know that in Ukraine people put spider ornaments on their Christmas trees?”

Aiden was still recovering from Emma’s touch.

She kept talking, though, and Aiden was relieved. He wasn’t sure if he trusted anything he might say.

“The story is that a family let in a spider one cold day. The family didn't have enough money for ornaments for their tree, so the spider made huge webs to decorate the tree. Cool, right?"

"That's pretty cool," Aiden agreed.

"*Pretty* cool? It's like combining Halloween with Christmas, my two favorite holidays! Remember that picture book I had when I was little?"

"You had a lot of picture books," Aiden teased.

Emma wiggled her fingers. "Did I tell you I'm reading a book about tarantulas?"

"Um, why?"

Emma grinned at him.

Aiden wasn't much of a reader, but Emma was usually reading at least three books at once, and he loved hearing about the things she read. Even if it was about spiders.

Aiden ate more of his peppermint brownie, not really sure what else he was supposed to say. The Frank Sinatra Christmas album was playing, though it was hard to hear over all the grown-ups' chatter.

"In Iceland, on Christmas Eve, people give each other books and they spend the rest of the night cozied up reading. Doesn't that sound so snuggly? Someday I'll go to Iceland for the holidays. Or heck, maybe Australia? It's their summer when it's our winter. Want to come with?"

Aiden was trying to keep up with the conversation. "Sounds nice, but holidays in Briar Glen are pretty great, too."

Aiden and Emma looked around the room, grown-ups holding mugs of drinks, everyone dressed festively. Aiden could just see the Christmas tree by the front window. Its white lights blinked on and off, and Aiden felt as if he were being hypnotized.

"Briar Glen isn't going anywhere," Emma said.

"Huh?" Aiden said, tearing his eyes away from the tree.

"If we went somewhere else for Christmas. It's not like Briar Glen wouldn't be here waiting for us when we got back. I'm not sure where I'd go first, though. Maybe I'd start more locally and do a New York City holiday. I'd love to see the tree at Rockefeller Center someday. And all the window displays."

Emma noticed how quiet Aiden had become. "What's wrong?"

Aiden tried to put into words what he was feeling. "I just can't imagine spending Christmas anywhere else, you know? I've had every Christmas of my life here, and so has my mom, and her parents. It's what my family does."

"I think they would understand if you want to spend one Christmas somewhere else," Emma said, shrugging.

"No. I don't think so. And even if they did, it wouldn't feel right for me," Aiden said stubbornly.

"You say that now. Eventually you'll want to spend at least one Christmas somewhere else, won't you?"

"I can't. Even if I wanted to, Christmas is also the busiest time of year for Grandpa, and the rest of my family, and I couldn't just leave them like that."

Emma said gently, "Aiden, I don't think your family expects you to spend every Christmas in Briar Glen for the rest of your life."

"Well, maybe *I* do. It's how my family operates."

Emma sighed. "I hope someday you reconsider, because I don't plan on being in Briar Glen for every Christmas for the rest of my life."

"You don't?"

"Someday I'll probably want to get a job somewhere else and live somewhere else."

"You will?"

"I mean, probably!" Emma said. "There are so many good colleges out there, outside of Briar Glen—"

"College!" Aiden yelped. "Are you already thinking about it?"

"Of course I am!"

This was news to Aiden.

"It's never too early to start planning," Emma said.

"I disagree."

"Kerry figured out where she wanted to go to college in middle school. I might as well do the same." Emma added, "Not that Kerry is the reason I'm thinking about college."

"Right," Aiden said. It was obvious that he didn't believe her. Emma didn't really believe herself.

"I just don't think I could leave my family," Aiden said again. "They need me. To help with the business. It's what our family does, and has been doing, since before I was even born."

Emma blinked. "Maybe we should stop talking about it?"

Aiden felt shaky. He couldn't figure out which thought made him more nervous: Emma not being in Briar Glen for Christmas, or him not being in Briar Glen for Christmas.

"Hey, I know what you need," Emma said.

Before Aiden could ask where she was going, Emma walked to the counter and started talking to Lucy, who was helping her mom with drink orders. Lucy handed Emma a steaming mug, and Emma grabbed a candy cane from the bowl by the register.

"Here, take this." Emma unwrapped the candy cane and then stirred it in the mug of hot chocolate before handing it to Aiden.

She watched Aiden intently as he took a sip. "No marshmallows. And extra pepperminty. Okay?" she asked.

"I think so." Aiden still felt slightly peculiar.

Emma's dad angled himself through the crowd and stopped

when he got to Emma and Aiden. "There you are!" He adjusted his Santa hat. The room was starting to feel warm, despite the practically subzero temperatures outdoors. The Charlie Brown Christmas album was playing now.

Emma's dad looked at her and she said, "Don't!" Then she elbowed him. "I know. We played this album all the time when I was a baby."

"Mind reader!" Emma's dad said. "I can still picture you in this little red dress you wore your first Christmas. You were crawling around and your legs kept getting caught in the dress, and you were getting so frustrated, but you kept going—"

Emma flopped her dad's Santa hat over his eyes to make him stop talking.

He laughed, pulled the hat off, and gestured around the room. "What a good turnout!"

"Yeah!" Aiden said, happy to think about dogs and to stop thinking about the conversation he'd been having with Emma. "This will bring in so much money for the shelter. Plus, the dogs in the back are really cute."

"Has your foster gotten here yet?" Mr. Sherman asked.

"Not yet."

"You must be so excited to meet him!" he said.

Aiden nodded. He was. He'd gotten more used to fostering the dogs and watching them go to happy homes. His family was still looking for a dog of their own to adopt, and Aiden knew they'd find the right one when the time was ready.

"What are you kids drinking, by the way?" Mr. Sherman peered into Aiden's mug.

"Like you need to ask," said Emma, as she took a big gulp of her peppermint hot chocolate. Then she stirred Aiden's candy cane in his mug.

Her hand brushed against Aiden's, and even though their hands had touched a million times before, this somehow felt different, too. Everything felt a little different. And Aiden hadn't even left Briar Glen. Emma looked away from Aiden, and he busied himself by looking around the room again at everyone, then at the donation tin that was overflowing with money.

Aiden's parents waved at him from the rear of the café.

"I'll be back," Aiden murmured, wondering why his hand felt so warm.

Emma and her dad were discussing a documentary about deep-sea creatures that they'd recently watched together, and Emma smiled at Aiden, her eyes lingering on him for just a second longer than usual.

Aiden made his way to the back of the café, politely pushing himself past guests until he got to his parents.

"The last dog is here!" Aiden's mom said excitedly. "Our foster!"

Aiden looked down at the dog pen, realizing there was a new addition.

The dog was black with a white patch on its chest and seemed like some kind of shepherd-collie mix. One of his ears stuck up, while the other lay flat against his head. His whole body wiggled when he saw Aiden.

"Meet our new foster dog!" Aiden's dad said.

Aiden bent down and let the dog sniff and lick his face.

"Well, I guess he likes you," Aiden's mom said.

The dog now flopped on his back, and Aiden rubbed the white patch on his chest.

"Who is this little guy?" Emma had joined the group now, too, and she knelt next to Aiden.

Aiden was only slightly aware of how close he and Emma were; the dog had taken his attention away from almost anything else.

Emma rubbed the dog's belly now, and he looked at her, his tongue lolling. "All of your foster dogs have been sweet, but this one—"

She stopped talking as the dog licked her face. She giggled. "This one seems pretty special!"

As Aiden petted the dog, the conversation he'd just had with Emma about her someday moving away from Briar Glen slipped further and further into the recesses of his mind. He looked up at his parents, and he could tell they were thinking the same thing about the dog.

They had found the one.

And Emma was there for it.

7

EMMA

We mill around the market for a while, but my heart just isn't in it. The smell of roasting chestnuts and mulled cider and German sausages mixes with the smell of the fresh-cut wreaths, and it's making me queasy. Part of the queasiness might be due to seeing Aiden; it felt like I was having a conversation with someone I didn't know very well. Which, at this point, I guess I don't, and the realization hits me right in the stomach. And Sam saying "we," like he's been to my house a million times, him wanting to go to the winter festival, to enter the sledding race. The way Aiden looked at me. Or barely looked at me.

There's that dull pain in my chest again.

But the longer we walk, the more distant the whole conversation feels, and the less I want to think about any of it. Especially because Sam seems completely unaffected by our visit to the market and seeing Aiden. Sam talks about snowboarding and tells me about the time there was a blizzard, and his family had canned soup for Christmas dinner, and since then he's never been able to eat tomato soup.

I'm trying hard to concentrate on what he's saying, but I'm grateful when my mom stops by a stand selling scarves made from local sheep's wool. She rubs the soft, thick fabric between her fingers. The scarf is a lavender purple, my favorite color, with little tassels. She says, "I know it's warmer in the city than here, but I still worry about you being cold since you walk everywhere."

"It's okay," I manage. "All the walking helps."

"Besides, Mrs. Sherman, I promise you," Sam chimes in, "I'll never let your daughter get cold."

Ordinarily such a statement from Sam would make me feel all melty, but it's like he's saying it from far away, from the opposite side of a tunnel, and I can't say anything back.

My mom smiles. "That's very sweet, but I still think she needs a new scarf. This one is much thicker." She's distracted, too.

"Mom, the one I have is fine," I say, thinking of the tattered blue-and-white striped scarf I've had for as long as I can remember. I think of all the winters I wore it sledding, ice-skating, going to school, walking around Briar Glen . . . all things I did with Aiden.

My dad and the vendor, a middle-aged man, come over to us. "See anything that you like?" the vendor asks.

"This is beautiful," my mom says, the lavender scarf still between her fingers.

The vendor beams. "Thank you."

My dad, who wants to make conversation with anyone and everyone, says, "You ever had goats? When I retire, I'm going to get goats."

The vendor seems confused. "Just sheep."

My dad tells the vendor about an article he read about the benefits of goat cheese, and the vendor listens politely.

My mom walks around, browsing, now holding the lavender scarf.

Sam touches an orange scarf. "We could get matching scarves!" he says, elbowing me.

"What a cute idea!" my mom says from a nearby rack.

"Oh, I was joking," Sam says, picking up the orange scarf between his index finger and thumb as if it might bite. "These aren't really my . . . style."

My dad and the vendor have stopped talking, and both seem like they want to say something to Sam. I feel a wave of embarrassment wash over me, like the wave of embarrassment I felt when Sam talked about not being an animal guy, but I'm not sure who the feeling is for, or how to get rid of it.

"The scarves are . . . really nice," I say awkwardly to the vendor.

The vendor's smile is gone as he squints at Sam. "These scarves are made from sheep from my own farm."

"They're incredible," my mom says, protectively clutching the lavender scarf in her hands. She looks at Sam now, too, clearly waiting for him to say something.

"Oh, they're amazing. I'm just not really a big fan of scarves," Sam says, though I'm not sure how genuine he's being. "Right, Emma? Have you ever seen me in a scarf?"

He laughs his usual easy laugh, but no one joins the laughter. Even me.

But Sam keeps going: "Besides, can you imagine us showing up at Easton in matching scarves? We don't want to be *that* couple, do we?"

I feel like everyone is staring daggers at me. "How long have you been making scarves?" I ask, trying to deflect Sam's questions, trying to somehow apologize to the vendor, but I'm not sure if it's working.

"The farm belonged to my grandparents," he says flatly, the warmth from his voice gone. "We've raised generations of sheep."

I look to my parents for help. My dad has said all he has to say about goats. My mom has always been good at smoothing over awkward moments, but she's not meeting my eyes.

"That's really cool," I say, trying and failing to make things normal. "I've always wanted to learn how to knit."

"You have?" Sam asks skeptically.

I've always wanted to learn how to do everything, and I did check out a beginner's guide to knitting from the library last year, and I did want to start a knitting club. But I'm not sure how passionately I ever felt about it.

"Yes," I say plainly.

Other customers have shown up at the booth, and the vendor starts to walk away. "I'll take the scarf," my mom says quickly. My dad nods in agreement before wandering off again.

"You don't have to do that," I say, putting my hand on hers, the overwhelm of seeing Aiden still stinging, and the way Sam just acted weighing me down like a pile of rocks.

"I know, but I want to," she says. And I know there's no use trying to argue with her.

My mom pays the vendor, whose smile has returned. We leave the tent, but everything feels off-kilter. My mom wraps the scarf around my neck.

"Thank you," I say, giving her a tight hug, trying to stabilize myself. "For everything."

She pulls away and gazes at me tenderly. "It's a beautiful scarf. On my beautiful daughter."

"Mom, stop, you're going to make me cry." And it's true; I already feel my eyes watering, even though I can't pinpoint why.

My mom swipes at her own eyes.

Sam watches us curiously. He puts out his hand for me to hold but doesn't say anything about my moment with my mom, or about the scarf, or about what he said to the vendor.

And, for once, I'm okay with his silence.

When we get home, the house is filled with the smell of baking chocolate gingerbread. As I remove my boots, I take deep breaths.

"You okay?" Sam asks, taking off his boots next to me. "You've barely said a word since we left the market."

"I'm okay, just sniffling. And I'll be even better once I eat some of that gingerbread!" I say with a grin, trying to bring back some levity.

"You and your sweet tooth," Sam teases. "I'm not a huge fan of desserts."

"I know, but my mom and dad have been making the same brownies since forever. You'll try those at least, won't you?"

The brownies were always Aiden's favorite dessert. I wonder how many he's eaten over the years. I feel even more dizzy now.

Sam kisses my forehead. "Maybe."

My parents have already hung up their coats, and they're in

the other room, straightening some of the presents under the Christmas tree. I think about previous Christmases, all the presents I opened under the tree. The time Aiden and I both got new Hot Wheels sets, and we played forever, our cars driving up and down new roads, forging new paths.

More ghosts.

Kerry pokes her head around the corner of the room, holding a whisk, flour on her forehead. “Want to help me make some sugar cookies?”

I yelp, startled out of my reverie, and Sam looks up from his phone, glancing between Kerry and me.

“I thought you guys already made them?” I remember the sadness I felt when I realized my family had baked the cookies without me.

“Yeah, well, maybe I wanted to bake some more,” she says impatiently. The gesture surprises me.

“Wait. You’re being a nice big sister?” I say teasingly. I want to give her a hug, but we don’t really do a lot of hugs, and I don’t want to ruin the moment. I hope Sam is witnessing this kindness from my older sister, but he’s scrolling.

“Don’t tell anyone,” Kerry says. “But, really, I could actually use your help.” She disappears back around the corner again.

I’m warm, and it’s not just from the oven.

"Want to bake some cookies?" I ask Sam eagerly. "I know, I know, you don't like desserts. But baking cookies is different than eating them. Did you know that Americans typically consume around twenty-six Christmas cookies each year?"

Cookies! Cookies will make everything feel normal again, right?

Sam says, "That's probably more Christmas cookies than I've ever eaten in my life. And besides, decorating cookies isn't really my thing. My parents never bake, and I don't want to ruin your sister-bonding moment."

He grins at me, but I feel my eagerness fading away. "Oh, so what are you going to do instead?"

"Would it be weird if I took a nap?" he asks, yawning dramatically. "I didn't sleep great last night. I think it's almost too quiet here."

"Emma!" my sister calls from the kitchen. "A little help?"

"I guess it is pretty different," I say, giving him the benefit of the doubt. I think back to when I first met Sam, how sweet he was showing me around Easton, around the city, but how overwhelmed I felt by its differences from Briar Glen.

"Thanks, Emma." He gives me a peck on the cheek.

He walks up the stairs, and I try to figure out why I'm feeling what I'm feeling. *Cookies*, I think again. *Cookies will make everything feel normal.*

"*There* you are," Kerry says as I step into the kitchen. "I was starting to regret my momentary kindness."

"Very funny," I say, but there's no humor in my voice.

"What's with you?" Kerry looks up from tightening her apron. "Also, where is your Prince Charming?"

"More like Sleeping Beauty. He's going to take a nap."

"I think you might actually be dating an eighty-year-old."

I don't respond.

"You all right? Something you want to talk about?" she asks.

I grab an apron of my own. "What would I want to talk about?"

Kerry's whisk is in midair. "Seriously? There are obviously like seven hundred things on your mind."

"Maybe seven hundred and one," I admit, my head spinning again. "But I don't know if I'm ready to talk about it yet. I think I'm still trying to figure some things out."

Kerry nods. "Got it. Well, if you want to talk about it or whatever, I could be that person you talk to." She laughs at her own awkward phrasing. "You know what I mean."

I chuckle, then look around the kitchen, which is covered in mixing bowls, a sheet full of chocolate gingerbread cookies, and Tupperware containers.

"Don't just stand there!" Kerry dusts the rolling pin with flour.

"Can you take the cookies off the baking sheet? Then you can get started on yours."

I follow her directions, carefully lifting the cookies off the sheet with a spatula, then slide them onto a plate decorated with reindeer. I keep my mind on the task, trying not to let my attention wander.

Kerry and I work in silence for a few minutes until she says, "So, if you're not ready to talk yet, want to hear about my morning? I ran into Luna. You remember her, right?"

"Luna! Duh, of course I do," I say. There's no way I'd ever forget Kerry's high school girlfriend. They dated for almost two years, and I rarely saw Kerry without Luna. "Where did you see her?"

"She was at the grocery store, buying more vanilla. Turns out I'm not the only one helping her parents bake." As she talks, she rolls out the sugar cookie dough on a baking sheet.

"That must have been bizarre."

"Bizarre? Nah, it's been so long."

"Why *did* you guys break up?" It was a question I had asked her at least a million times—Luna was usually nicer to me than Kerry, and ten-year-old me had more than once imagined what it would be like if Luna were my sister instead of Kerry—but Kerry had only ever told me I wouldn't understand.

"I told you, it was complicated."

I put my spatula down, all the chocolate gingerbread cookies loaded onto a plate. I inhale deeply, momentarily distracted. "C'mon, that's what you told me when I was a kid." Then I pout and try to whimper, but I snort instead, and Kerry starts laughing.

"Yep, you're such a big grown-up teenager now," she teases, whacking me with an oven mitt. "I guess it really wasn't that complicated. We just weren't each other's person anymore."

"And?"

She slides the sugar cookie dough to me. "And it just didn't feel right anymore. When we first fell in love, it felt like . . ." She trails off, then smiles wistfully. "It was like nothing I'd ever felt before. I suddenly understood why there were so many songs about falling in love. The fireworks, the way my heart ached for her. But, well, we changed so much over those two years, and we just kind of grew apart."

I think about Sam's eyes, the way he looks at me. I can't imagine not ever getting chills when he touches me, him not beaming every time I walk into a room.

But I remember something else. "Sam and I haven't told each other we love each other yet."

Kerry is flipping through our family cookbook, some of its pages crusted together, until she lands on the page for the giant chocolate cake roll my mom has been making forever. There are chocolate smudges all over the recipe. She looks up at me. "You haven't been together for very long," she says wisely. "But *do* you love him? That doesn't seem like something you'd keep to yourself."

I laugh uncomfortably. "I'm not sure yet?" I think about the electricity that seems to flow between my hands and Sam's hands whenever they touch. I feel a little grin trying to spread across my face.

"You seem pretty smitten," Kerry scoffs.

"Yeah. I guess I'm just not sure if we're there yet. At the love stage."

"Are you sure you're not just smitten with the idea of having a boyfriend?"

I pick up a cookie cutter and start cutting nutcracker, mitten, and star shapes into the dough. I dig through the tin of cookie cutters, grab a candy cane shape, and immediately put it back down again. "That's silly. I like *Sam*."

"What is it about *him*?" she persists.

"He's driven, he loves school, he knows all these things about New York. Things that I'd never know. Things that he gets since it's where he was born and where he grew up."

"So he's basically the complete opposite of Aiden."

"What does Aiden have to do with anything?" I snap.

"He's your best friend," Kerry says, looking at me, brow furrowed. "It's just . . . interesting how different he is from Sam."

"Weren't we talking about you and Luna? Can we go back to that?"

"Just an observation!" Kerry says defensively. "Anyway, I don't know. It's like, Luna and I clicked, and then we unclicked. The more I got into dancing and performing, the further away she seemed to be from me. She supported me, but she didn't really understand it. She didn't really understand me . . . anymore."

"Luna didn't understand you? But you guys always seemed so happy."

"That's the thing. We weren't *not* happy. I realized couples don't always break up because both people are miserable. Sometimes people just grow and change. We started as a tree, a solid trunk in the ground, but our branches went different ways."

"But you loved each other."

"Sure. We still do love each other. We probably always will. But it isn't the kind of love to sustain a relationship."

"Sam is a good guy." I sigh, feeling confused and off-balance. "I think we love each other. It's not like we have to say it to know it . . . right?"

Kerry shrugs. "You tell me."

"At the market, when he was talking to one of the vendors, he was so . . . not rude, necessarily. But maybe a little condescending?"

"What happened?" She picks up the cinnamon Red Hots and adds them to the nutcrackers as buttons. I add rainbow sprinkles.

I think back to the exchange he had with the wool vendor. "He was trying to be friendly, or make a joke, or something. But it came out almost like he was mocking the guy selling scarves."

Kerry pauses mid-sprinkle. "Ouch. How did that go over with Mom and Dad? How did that go over with *you*?"

"I don't know. We didn't really talk about it. He was weird with Aiden, too."

Kerry still hovers the jar of sprinkles over a star-shaped cookie.

I remember the way Sam talked to Aiden, overfamiliarly, the way Aiden barely looked at me. "Sam wants to be in the sled race at the winter festival, too. And I guess maybe it's . . . challenging having him here."

And seeing Aiden.

I continue unsurely, "I didn't realize how big of a deal it would be bringing Sam to Briar Glen. These different parts of my life are . . ."

"Crashing into each other?" Kerry offers.

"Something like that. Sam says he wants to learn about me—about my *origin story*, as he calls it. But I guess I didn't think about how much of that origin story includes Aiden," I say, the realization hitting me.

"Of course. Aiden's your best friend," Kerry says again. She slides our tray of sugar cookies into the oven and then brushes off her hands.

"He is."

I think.

"So when are you going to hang out with him?" She starts pulling ingredients out to make the icing for the sugar cookies. We usually do one batch of sugar cookies with sprinkles and the other batch with icing.

Hang out with Aiden? Something I used to do all the time. Something I haven't done in months.

"I'm not sure."

"You saw him at the market today, and at Cup o' Jo last night, and you didn't make any plans?"

I groan. "I didn't even see him at Cup o' Jo, but outside of it. It was so strange. Mack was more excited to see me than Aiden. He said something about how I got everything I wanted."

"What's that supposed to mean?"

"I don't really know. He apologized today, but then I had to apologize, too, for not really being in touch, and he said he was sorry, too, and—"

"What do you mean 'not really being in touch'? You guys used to talk, like, a hundred times a day."

"It's been different since I've been at Easton. We barely talk."

Kerry raises an eyebrow at me. "And why is that?"

I think about the meaningless emojis we've sent back and forth, my pictures of pretty sunsets reflected against Manhattan's skyscrapers. His pictures to me of Mackerel, Briar Glen's first snowfall of the season, a new sled his grandpa had made. Conversations I'd have with someone I don't know very well. Not someone I've known since he was afraid of Santa, someone whose dog knows his way to my house.

"We didn't really part on great terms." I sigh. "I kind of . . . left without saying goodbye?"

Kerry drops the egg she's holding, and it explodes all over the counter. "Um, first of all, why, and second of all, why am I just hearing about this now?"

"I dunno . . . I guess . . . if I talked about it, then that would make it real."

"So you just avoided the whole thing?" She cleans up the egg, then cracks another egg, separating the egg white into a mixing bowl.

"I know."

"Why would you—"

"It's just complicated, okay?"

"Hey, that's my line." She gestures to the mixer, which is ready to be turned on.

I flip the switch and the mixer starts whirring, whisking the royal icing.

"He was . . . I don't even know. He wasn't supportive, when I told him I got into Easton."

"Emma . . ." my sister says gently.

"But then he got quiet when I told him I was going, and then I decided to start at Easton early, and I didn't know how to say goodbye to him—I didn't *want* to say goodbye to him—"

"Emma—"

"And the texts we've been sending to each other have been so fake, and I didn't even tell him about Sam, and I didn't exactly tell Sam about Aiden, either—"

"Emma!" my sister says more urgently now.

"Oh!"

I snap back to the present and find that the icing I was whisking has escaped the mixing bowl and is flying everywhere. I quickly turn off the mixer. There's icing dripping from the front of the refrigerator, the cabinets; there's even some in Kerry's hair.

"Oops," I say bashfully. "Sorry . . . I guess I was distracted."

"Ya think?"

We wipe up the icing from around the kitchen, and Kerry washes it out of her hair.

"Now, what were you saying about Aiden?" she continues, wiping down the counter.

"I guess I was saying that I need to talk to him."

"That might be a good idea. You can't avoid him your entire holiday break. And he'll be at the party tomorrow, won't he?" She bends down to check the cookies in the oven.

Aiden. In my house. Sam. In my house. Together.

"I think so?"

"So just talk to him," Kerry says matter-of-factly. "I know you miss him. It's obvious he misses you."

"It is?"

"Emma, c'mon. It's *Aiden*. How long have you guys known each other?"

She's right. It's Aiden. He's been to my house hundreds of times. Thousands. So what if Sam will be there, too?

"I do have to ask, though . . ." Kerry begins. "Did Mom ever tell you how she thinks that someday you and Aiden will be together?"

"What?" I'm breathless for a second. "Is she telling that to everyone?"

"Nah. Just me. And probably Dad."

"That's . . . that's . . ." I struggle for the right word again. "Preposterous!"

"Good SAT word."

"I'm here with Sam. Sam is my boyfriend."

But am I trying to convince Kerry . . . or myself?

"He's not perfect," I finally say. But I don't know who I'm talking about.

"Listen, I'm not one to tell you what to do—"

"Since when?"

"Very funny," she says with a smirk. "I'm not going to tell you what to do, except for this one thing."

"And what's that?"

She puts her hands on my shoulders. "Follow your heart."

I look at her for a moment, wonder where this version of Kerry has been hiding all these years. "Anything else?"

"That's it," she says.

"You make it sound so simple and easy."

"It is." She pulls the baking sheet out of the oven.

We both admire the lumpy and unevenly decorated cookies. "What do you think?" Kerry asks.

"They're one of a kind. And perfect."

8

AIDEN

It snows overnight—icy, wet snow—which means fewer customers at the market. Grandpa says his bones hurt in this kind of weather, so it's just Dad and me. And Mack, tired from playing in the snow earlier, who stays in his dog bed.

Despite the weather, I'm on edge, worried Emma might show up again. Or worse yet, Emma and Sam.

I'm dusting snow off the wooden planters when Dad claps me on the back. "You know those are waterproof, right? They're meant to be outdoors?"

"Sorry."

"No need to apologize." He puts his hands in his coat pockets. "Something on your mind?" he asks, not making eye contact with me.

I avoid his eyes, too, look out at the booth across from ours, which is selling homemade jam. "I guess."

"I know it's hard to believe, but I was young once." He turns to face me. "If there is something you're going through or something on your mind, then I might be able to give advice?"

"Thanks, Dad."

We stand there in silence, and he seems like he's about to walk away, but I say, "It's really odd having Emma back in Briar Glen again."

Dad nods, shuffles his feet. "Probably odd having her boyfriend here, too. And did I hear something about him entering the sled race?"

I wince at the word *boyfriend*, and at the reminder about the race.

"With one of our sleds," I mutter.

"Ah. Does the boyfriend have anything to do with why you and Emma haven't spoken much?"

"Wait, who told you about us not talking?"

He shuffles his feet again and chuckles. "No one needed to tell me. Anyone with any kind of sense would figure it out."

"Dad, what are you talking about?" I rub my head.

"You've barely brought up her name since she left for school. And I haven't heard you FaceTiming her, which I thought I'd hear every day when she moved."

"She didn't move!" I say quickly. "She's just at boarding school."

"Still. I thought we'd hear about her, hear from her. And it's been quiet. *You've* been quiet."

Now I'm at a loss for words, further proving his point. "I didn't even know about Sam until the other day."

Dad is quiet this time. "I was a teenager in love once, too." He shrugs.

"Who said anything about love?" I can't look at him.

He shrugs again. "Sometimes you don't need to say anything about it at all."

"Thanks?" I say uncertainly.

"Seems like a million years ago." He stares off into the distance.

"Dad?" I say when he's still quiet.

He shakes his head, back in the present moment. "I've been there, is all. Briar Glen is a small town, and now I'm sure it seems like Emma's boyfriend is everywhere. The sled race, the party tonight—"

"Think I could skip the party?"

"Aiden, you don't mean that."

"I don't?"

"No. No matter what, Emma is your friend. Right?"

I nod reluctantly. Sam or no Sam, I'm not missing an opportunity to see Emma. Maybe we can actually have a real conversation.

"Still, though, the pain. I remember it. I know it," Dad says.

A customer browses, picks up a snowman decoration, and Dad walks toward her. He helps the customer, and I stand there, unable to move, wondering what else Dad knows.

When we get home, Mackerel and I go up to my room. He collapses dramatically in his bed.

"Tough day at the office?" I ask, scratching the white spot on his chest with one hand while I dig around in my laundry basket with the other. Finally, at the bottom of the basket, I find the goofy reindeer sweatshirt I wear every holiday season. I squeeze the antlers, and they squeak. I pull it over my head, trying not to remember who gave it to me.

I catch my reflection in the mirror hanging from the back of my door, and I look ridiculous. Plus, my hair is sticking to my head in a funny way from wearing my hat at the market. I run my fingers through my hair, but now I just look like I have bedhead. I run my fingers through my hair a few more times, muttering, "It's just a holiday party. It's just a holiday party." A party I've been to a million times, at a house I've been to a million times. But, as I smooth down my hair, I mutter, "A party with Emma's boyfriend."

My hair is as good as it's going to get, so I step back from the mirror, and then remember my sweatshirt. I've worn it to every party for the last few years, ever since Emma gave it to me, but I wonder if I should change. I briefly wonder what Sam is wearing.

I dig through my basket again, pulling out a wrinkled flannel shirt, just as Grandma shouts up the stairs, "Aiden! Let's go! I'm roasting down here!"

"Ma, remember what I said about overheating in your coat?" Mom says gently.

"I wouldn't overheat if the people in this family weren't always running late!"

Mom sighs, then says tensely, "Aiden, we need to go!"

I give the flannel shirt in my hand one last glance before I toss it back in my laundry basket. Ridiculous reindeer sweatshirt it is.

"Wish me luck," I say to Mack, though I don't know what luck has to do with anything.

"About time," Grandma mumbles as I walk down the stairs and into the mudroom. Dad catches my eye before we head out into the night air.

The Shermans' house is just a few streets away, but I've managed to avoid walking Mackerel this way since June, and it feels a bit like I'm visiting someplace from my childhood that I haven't been in years.

We round the corner onto their street, and their house twinkles off in the distance.

"I don't want to stay too long," I blurt out as we get closer.

Everyone stops walking, and we all bump into one another.

"Why?" Mom asks. "I thought you'd want to spend time with Emma."

"I do," I say. "I just . . . didn't sleep well last night."

Grandpa says, "So? Not like a lack of sleep ever stopped you from hanging out with Emma before."

I look at Dad, but he's quiet, and just gives me a knowing smile.

We all start walking again.

"I think I'm entering the sled race." I don't realize the words are going to come out of my mouth until they do, and we all bump into one another again. I instantly wonder if I can take the words back. But no. I can't. I won't.

"What?" my parents and grandparents all say at once.

"The sled race. I want to do it," I say. "I've never lived anywhere but Briar Glen, I help Grandpa and Dad sell sleds, and I haven't raced in two years!"

I feel my parents and grandparents having silent conversations around me. "Are you sure that's a good idea?" Mom asks. "You're not doing it to prove anything, are you?"

I give her a sharp look. "What would I need to prove?"

Mom puts her hands up. "It was just a question!"

"If you want to," Dad says. "Just make sure you're doing it for the right reasons."

"Guys, it's just a sled race. Think how good it'll be for business." I cup my hands around my mouth, mimicking a megaphone. "'Aiden Cooper-Gallo, out on his grandpa's handcrafted sled!'"

They all look at me, confused.

"Besides," I continue, "Grandma is always telling me to face my fears."

"He's not wrong," she says. "Only thing to fear is fear itself."

"Yeah, and another wrist injury!" Mom adds.

"Mom!" And then, more gently, "I'm not a little kid. I can handle it. I can handle a lot more things than I think I can."

"That's the spirit!" Grandma says, nudging Grandpa, who joins in saying, "Yeah, son, you're right. You can handle a lot more than you give yourself credit for."

"Thanks?" I turn toward my parents.

"You're right, you're right," Mom says. "He's a big boy. Maybe sometimes I forget how big." She wraps me in a hug, and I protest at first, but it's half-hearted, and soon she's embracing me.

"I still don't think we should leave the party early," she says.

"Why?" But I'm distracted, already wondering if the sled race is a huge mistake.

Am *I trying to prove something? And if so, to whom?*

We all start walking again.

"You want to leave the party early, you leave the party early!" Grandma says, then turns to her daughter. "He's a grown boy."

"I know, Ma," Mom says. "I just think it'd be polite if he stayed for a bit. Though this may be the first time I've ever told him he can't leave the Sherman house. You know how many epic all-day playdates Emma and Aiden used to have when they were little. I practically had to drag him out of their house sometimes. And it sure didn't stop as you got older! Then I think you were there even more, or Emma at our house. Not that I ever minded."

I don't say anything.

"You must miss Emma," Grandma says.

"Martha, didn't you just say he's a grown boy?" Grandpa chides. "Leave the kid—er, guy—alone."

"It's fine!" I say quickly, ready to stop talking and thinking about Emma.

Which will be hard, because we've just gotten to her house. In their front yard I see the old Santa and reindeer decorations that were Emma's mom's when she was a kid. The same plastic candy canes that Emma's family have put out every year line the path to the porch, and I feel a twist somewhere inside my chest.

Every inch of the porch is covered in lights—even the railings—and Grandpa and Dad climb the porch steps, commenting on the kinds of bulbs.

I walk up the stairs behind them, and it feels like a dream. I haven't set foot on these steps or inside the Sherman house in six months.

There's a huge fluffy wreath hanging from the front door, with a COME ON IN! sign taped to it.

Even though the door is closed, I hear the laughter and chatter of party guests, a folksy version of "Rudolph the Red-Nosed Reindeer" playing over the speakers.

Grandma opens the door, and I have to catch my breath. Stepping over the threshold makes everything feel like a dream again. The space is familiar—so familiar—but also seems so . . . strange.

There are little kids running around from the entryway through the dining room and out into the living room, and the house smells like a mixture of sugar cookies, chocolate, mulled cider, and fresh Christmas tree.

My parents and grandparents are already making their way to the dining room, greeting friends and neighbors on the way. The table is covered with all kinds of desserts, including a three-tiered tray stacked with chocolate shortbread, my favorite brownies in the world, and sugar cookies. The cookies are haphazardly decorated, spicy cinnamon candies and sprinkles of all colors dashed across them. Emma made these.

I feel frozen in place, until someone bumps into my back. I turn, and it's Kerry, holding a hand soap refill for the powder room.

"Hey, stranger!" she says. "I heard from Mom and Dad that you haven't been here in months."

I duck sheepishly. "Things got busy, you know?"

Kerry looks at me doubtfully. "Uh-huh," she says, heading into the powder room. "Help yourself to food and drinks," she says over her shoulder. "There's too much of everything!"

I don't have an appetite at the moment, though, so I enter the living room.

I see Emma before she sees me. She stands by the Christmas tree, beaming, but I can't see at who. She's wearing a long green dress and a red ribbon headband, and she looks . . .

The crowd parts, and I see Sam. That's who Emma was smiling at. I turn to leave, but it's too late.

"Aiden!" Emma calls.

I close my eyes, take a deep breath, and turn back around. She looks so happy, and her joy still has that magnetic effect on me, and I find myself walking over to where she's standing.

She's grinning, like she's delighted to see me, like when I saw her at the market wasn't totally uncomfortable, like my first encounter with Sam outside Cup o' Jo went smoothly. Like June never happened.

"I'm so glad you came!" she says. She throws her arms around my neck. The antler on my sweatshirt squeaks, and she's hugging me so tight that I can feel her laughing. Her skin is so soft, and her hair still has that same fruity smell. It's the first time we've touched or even been this close to each other in months, and my senses feel a bit overloaded. Yet I don't want to let go of her. I want to pretend there is no Sam standing inches away from us.

She pulls back from me, and she's wearing her boots, so we're exactly the same height, looking right into each other's eyes. Her eyes are locked on mine, and her smile falters for just a second.

"It's so good to see you!" she says. Then she grabs my hand, and I feel my breath catch in my throat. "Have you been wearing the gloves?"

I know she asked me a question, but I can't think of the answer with her hand on mine, so I say, "I, uh, forgot where I put them."

Emma lets go of my hand. "His hands are always freezing!" she says, turning to face Sam. Then she looks at me again. "It's really so good to see you."

It's amazing to see you, too, I think.

Emma hooks her arm onto Sam's elbow and the spell breaks,

and I instantly remember Sam saying "we." I feel my jaw clench.

"I'm so glad I saw that flier at your tent yesterday. I can't wait for the winter festival and sled race! I've been snowboarding pretty much since I could walk," Sam says, winking at me.

I hate winks.

"It's not really a race, remember?" I say through gritted teeth. "Just for fun. But, uh, I think I'm going to enter the race, too. I mean, I'm going to do it."

I don't know who seems more surprised, Emma or Sam.

"A-are you sure?" Emma asks. "What about what happened—"

"It was two years ago! I'm over it," I lie. I don't want Sam to know about when I fell off my sled.

Emma knows I'm lying.

Sam laughs. "Well, that's funny timing, isn't it?"

I glare at him. "What is *that* supposed to mean?"

Emma gives me a pleading look. And it's happening. I haven't seen her in six months, she left in June without saying goodbye, but I can tell what she wants me to do without her even asking. She wants me to be nice to Sam. And then I wonder: *Is that why she was so friendly? The hug, her telling me it was so good to see me? Was it all a performance for Sam?*

It hurts, it physically hurts my chest, but I paste a smile on my face and say, "So, what else do you have planned while you're visiting Briar Glen? You saw the tree and the town square."

"Yep, saw all that my first night here. And Cup o' Jo, of course."

Hearing the café name coming from his mouth is more salt on an open wound.

"Aiden's family has been hanging up the lights in the town square and around Briar Glen since his mom was little," Emma says. She looks so proud, so happy, and it's contagious, that feeling.

Sam puts his arm around Emma's shoulder, and I try to keep smiling, but the ache I felt in my chest has now spread to my face. "She showed me all around the market, too. Well, you remember! I have an excellent Briar Glen tour guide."

"You do. She's the best," I say, looking at Emma. The smile has died on my face, and everything hurts.

"I think the roasted chestnuts were even better than the ones I've had in the city," Sam says.

"Obviously," I say before I can stop myself.

"Emma's mom bought her the nicest scarf, too, made from local wool. I almost thought about us getting matching scarves, but we have a reputation to maintain, right, Emma?"

I look at Emma, waiting for some explanation of what Sam is talking about, but she just keeps smiling.

"And obviously the Christmas markets in the city are bigger, but this one was pretty cool, too," Sam goes on.

"Cool." I wonder how much longer I have to stand here.

"So I saw the town square, all decorated and lit up; and the tree; and the holiday market; Cup o' Jo; and Emma's house is like something on a holiday postcard; and there's the winter festival . . . What else do I need to do to complete my Briar Glen bucket list?" Sam asks, tapping his chin. "Oh, I know—we should go ice-skating tomorrow."

"We should!" Emma agrees, wiggling out from under his arm.

"I've only ever ice-skated in the city, never at a smaller rink," Sam explains. "Could be fun."

"Yeah," Emma says, then turns to me. "You should come skating with us!"

I force myself to look at her again. "I should?"

"He should?" Sam echoes.

"This way you guys can get to know each other better!"

"Isn't that . . . what we're doing now?" Sam asks uncomfortably.

But Emma is so hopeful, so earnest, and she's Emma, so I say, "I'll think about it."

Emma's entire face lights up, and I know I'll put skates on my feet for her.

But then we all just stand there, until Emma says, “Did you know that the first ice skates were made out of bone?”

“Ew,” Sam says, just as I say, “Scandinavia?”

Emma is pleased. “You remember!”

I laugh. “You do bring it up every time we go skating.” My laugh dies. “Every time we *used* to go skating.”

Emma’s expression is pained.

“Oh, Emma, you should tell him about the time we went skating at Rockefeller Center,” Sam says.

“That was always one of your dreams, wasn’t it?” I ask. “To see the big tree and all?”

“You remembered that, too,” Emma says softly, looking at me.

“She’s such a good skater!” Sam says, ignoring what I just said, and what Emma just said.

“I know,” I say, but I’m looking at Emma.

“Hey, I like your sweatshirt,” Sam says, pointing.

Is he smirking at me?

“Thanks,” I say. And before I can stop the words from escaping, I add, “Your girlfriend gave it to me.”

Emma’s eyes widen for just a second. “How many years ago was that now? I’m glad it still fits you.”

I pull out the sweatshirt and examine it. “Just a couple years.”

"What a find," Sam remarks. "Where on earth did you get it, Emma?"

"Probably somewhere online, who knows."

"Yeah, I can't imagine you'd find that in a store in Briar Glen," Sam says. "Especially since your stores close so early. No offense!" he says, putting his hands up.

"It *is* pretty sleepy here," Emma says, forcing me to look at her as she leans against Sam.

"So?" I say stubbornly.

"It's different than the city," Sam explains. "There's always something to do there. Someone is always having a party, or there's always an art exhibit or book event or a movie screening, or we can eat at a restaurant from a different country every day of the week. Every day of the month, even."

"Aiden, when you visit me, we have to go to this dim sum place," Emma says excitedly. "It's amazing."

"When I visit you?" I hear myself repeat.

"When is he visiting you?" Sam asks, and I see a small crack in his grinning facade.

"I don't know!" Emma says. "Hopefully soon," she says, looking at me, eyes wide with optimism.

"I'll have to think about it." I remember the ice-skating invitation, and Emma's pleading look before, her mental request to be nice to Sam. I also remember her arms around me in that hug, which I again wonder if it was all for show. For Sam.

"You've been to the city before, right, Aiden?" Sam asks, like he's talking to a child.

I will not tell him the truth—that I've never been—and give him any satisfaction, so I ask Emma, "Did your parents make their brownies?"

"You know it. I hope there are some left."

Sam says, "Let me go check. I'm going to grab some coffee, too. Should I get anything else?"

"I'm good," I say, hearing the honey-sweet fake kindness dripping out of my voice.

"Do you mind getting something for me?" Emma asks.

"Sure, what would you like?"

Emma is flustered. "How about some water? And some brownies. And maybe something else from the dessert tray, too?"

"You trust me to choose a dessert for you?" Sam asks.

"Sure. Surprise me."

"Anything for you." Sam kisses her forehead, and I look away so fast I make myself dizzy. But when I look back, Sam is walking away.

Emma and I are alone. Well, as alone as we can be in the middle of a holiday party. Someone bumps into me, and I'm pushed closer to Emma. She puts one of her hands on my arm to steady me, and before

I even realize what I'm doing, I rest my hand against hers. We both look at my hand on her hand. I look into her eyes, which I've done a million times, but it seems so different after not doing it for months.

"I've missed you," she says in such a low voice I'm not sure I've heard her correctly.

"I have, too," I say, also in a low voice. But I miss the Emma I used to know, and I'm not totally sure who this person standing with me really is.

She pulls her hand away from mine and steps back, and I already want to touch her again. "New York is an amazing city."

"So I've heard."

"I know, you're not really a city person," Emma points out. "You haven't been there yet. I don't mean that in a bad way. I haven't been a lot of places. A lot of people haven't been a lot of places. But I wish you would at least think about changing that. I think you'd really like the city."

"And why do you think that?" I ask doubtfully.

"Well, the music for one. There are shows and concerts everywhere. And all kinds of music, whatever you want. Heck, we could go see an opera!"

"We?" I can't help but say.

"Sure, you and me."

"And Sam?"

"And Sam what?"

"Would he be going with us to this opera?"

Emma's smile fades. "Oh, I don't know. Maybe."

We're quiet for a second. I study the Christmas tree, and I see one of my family's sled ornaments. I fiddle with another ornament—a ball, with a piece of ribbon inside. "I remember this one." We made them in kindergarten. The ribbon inside is how tall we were.

She puts her hand on the ornament, too. "Have you ever taken the ribbon out to see how much you've grown?"

"I tried once, but my parents freaked out. They didn't want me to break it."

Emma taps on the ornament. "But it's plastic. And the top screws off."

"Listen, sometimes it's just better if I don't ask questions."

She laughs.

I touch another ornament. A paper gingerbread cookie, with Emma's picture in place where the face should be.

"I forgot about this one," I say. "First grade?"

Emma examines the picture. "Yeah. I can tell because my front tooth is missing."

"You're so cute."

Emma seems surprised.

"In the picture," I say quickly.

Emma says, "Yes, of course. Do you still have your gingerbread cookie ornament?"

"Yep, at the back of the tree, right where it's supposed to be."

"Aiden!" Emma laughs. "You were adorable."

"Um, thanks," I say, my face feeling hot.

"Aw, you still are."

My face feels even hotter. "Still am what?"

Emma looks at me, eyes wide. "Adorable," she says as more people pass by looking for snacks. "Maybe we should go somewhere else? It feels crowded over here, doesn't it? And I bet Sam is looking for us."

I follow Emma away from the tree, out of the living room and to the entryway. Except we hit a small traffic jam of people taking off their coats and are stuck in the doorway.

Jack is helping Lucy out of her coat, and they both wave to us.

"You might want to move away from the doorway," Jack says.

"Huh?" Emma and I say at the same time.

Lucy points up, and I don't know how I didn't see it before.

"Okay, that was definitely not there earlier today," Emma says, looking at the mistletoe. Which she and I are standing directly under.

As if to prove the point, Jack gently holds Lucy's face. She leans forward, and they kiss.

Emma and I stare at them, and then we both look up at the mistletoe again.

Jack and Lucy pull away from each other as Emma says, "I swear my parents must have just hung it!"

I look up again. "I definitely didn't see it when I came in."

We both stand there, staring at the top of the doorway. When I look down again, Emma is staring at me.

"What?" I ask nervously.

"Nothing!" she says.

Lucy and Jack finally make their way into the party.

Emma and I don't move, though.

"We should probably—" I start just as Emma says, "This is so silly. But it really is bad luck if you don't kiss someone when you're standing under mistletoe."

"Kiss?" I yelp.

"Oh, like I would just kiss your hand or something! Otherwise, that would be weird. And I have Sam!"

"Right, Sam."

"Aiden! Just, can I have your hand?"

"Um, okay? My right hand or my left hand?"

"Whichever one you want!"

I look at my hands. Emma is about to kiss one of them. This has become one of the most dreamlike holiday parties I've ever been to.

I put out my right hand slowly, and Emma takes it. She laughs. "I'm so superstitious, I'm sorry."

"I know." I think about all the cracks in the sidewalks we used to step over, how Emma would never let me pick up a penny if it was face down. But it's hard for me to concentrate, because Emma is holding my hand, and she's raising it to her mouth. She brings it closer to her face, and I feel her laughing, and then her lips are on my hand for a split second, but that second is enough to set off fireworks throughout my body, and I hear myself gasp.

And then I hear someone say, "What's going on?"

Emma drops my hand like it's on fire, and really it does feel pretty warm.

She turns, and Sam is there, holding a plateful of desserts, a water bottle, and a mug of something steaming. He's glaring at me. "What the heck?"

I can't speak, but Emma calmly says, "It's mistletoe."

"So that just gives you the right to kiss someone else?" he spits out.

"I kissed his hand," Emma says, crossing her arms. "It's mistletoe. It's bad luck not to kiss someone under it. And I only kissed Aiden's hand."

Sam's glare deepens, but that doesn't matter anymore. Emma kissed my hand. It wasn't a dream.

"Oh please," Sam says. "How would you feel if I kissed some girl's hand under some dumb plant?"

"It's not a dumb plant. Remember we learned about it when we were doing the mythology section in English class? And Aiden isn't just 'some guy,' by the way."

"Yeah, if he's so important to you, then why have you never mentioned his name to me once? I didn't even know he existed until, like, two days ago."

The warmth in my hand fades.

Emma's eyes dart over to me, but Sam goes on, talking to me now. "You heard me. I didn't know a single thing about you."

I'm about to tell him that I didn't know about him, either, but Emma says, "That's enough!"

Sam and I both whip our heads around to look at her.

"What I talk about, who I talk about, who I touch, is no one's business but my own!"

Sam rolls his eyes. "Chill out."

Emma's mouth hangs open for a moment. "Are you serious right now?"

"I don't know," Sam shoots back. "Are you?"

Emma puts her head in her hands. "I cannot even believe this is happening."

She looks at me, and I feel my power of speech coming back. "That was a pretty awful thing to say."

"So now you're speaking for her?" Sam shoots back. "Wow."

Emma looks back and forth between Sam and me.

My head is spinning. Emma kissed my hand, but her boyfriend didn't even know I existed. I didn't even know *he* existed. And he just told Emma to chill out.

I want to defend myself and I want to defend Emma, but I know she doesn't need my help. And the sting of knowing that she didn't talk about me for five months is starting to really burn.

"I think it's time for me to go," I say.

"What?" Emma says. "You just got here."

"Does it matter? I kind of feel like I don't even exist."

"No!" Emma says desperately. "You do exist. Of course you do. This has all gotten way out of hand."

Sam snorts. "Hand. Yeah, sure has."

Emma shakes her head. "I don't even . . ."

"I think this is between you and Sam," I say, not being able to use the word *boyfriend*. "I need to feed Mackerel. You know how he gets."

Emma looks at me suspiciously. "You didn't feed him before you left?"

She knows I'm lying.

"I guess it slipped my mind."

"And you just remembered now?"

She knows.

"Yeah, I guess so."

She knows. But she didn't even mention you once to her boyfriend.

"If he needs to feed his dog, he needs to feed his dog," Sam says.

And that's when I realize I'm at my breaking point. This guy who didn't even know who I was is telling my best friend to chill out and is talking about *my dog* to Emma.

Emma knows I've hit my breaking point, too. "Can we please at least ice-skate tomorrow?"

It's such a ridiculous request given everything that happened in the last few minutes. But it's so ridiculous that maybe it'll somehow make things right.

"Sure," I say, wanting this conversation to end. "Okay."

"Great." Emma visibly relaxes. "How about eleven?"

"I'll see you tomorrow." I turn to go, not sure why I'm agreeing to go. Not sure of much of anything, really.

As I put on my coat, I hear Emma say, "Sam, you still up for ice-skating tomorrow?"

I don't bother with my gloves, and I'm out the door before I can hear his response.

DECEMBER, THREE YEARS AGO.

"Are you almost done?" Emma asked Aiden impatiently.

Aiden laughed and took one final sip of his peppermint hot chocolate, draining the mug. "Done."

"Finally!" Emma stood from her chair at Cup o' Jo and zipped up her coat.

Aiden stood, too, trying to keep up with Emma, but she was ready to go while he was still pulling on his hat. "Why are you in such a hurry?" he teased. "It's not like the ice is going to melt."

"You know the ice is better the earlier we get there."

"I know, I know." Aiden bumped his shoulder into Emma's playfully.

Jo was behind the counter, making a sandwich for a customer. "Have fun. I hope those hot chocolates keep you nice and warm!"

"Bye, Jo!" Emma called from the front door. "Thanks again!"

Emma and Aiden made their way to the ice rink, which was a few streets away from the town square. They passed stores adorned with wreaths and holiday window displays, and lights hung by Aiden's family.

"We should take Mackerel ice-skating with us sometime," Emma said.

Aiden chuckled. "I don't think they make skates in his size."

"Do you think he'd need ice skates? A lot of dogs know how to walk on ice instinctively."

Aiden pictured his dog sliding around on the ice.

Emma said, "Though thinking about him in ice skates is really cute."

They both pictured Mack with skates on his paws. "He'd hate that!" Aiden said.

"Do you think so? Is Mackerel capable of hating anything?"

"Squirrels. He hates squirrels."

"Oh yeah, I forgot about squirrels." Emma paused. "You know, the more I think about it, though, the more I feel like ice skates might insult him." She pictured it vividly now, and this time Mackerel was wearing a scarf and a winter parka. She giggled.

"What are you laughing at?" Aiden asked, trying to keep a straight face, having a similar vision as Emma's, but this one included Mackerel wearing goggles.

"He'd hate it!" Emma gasped, trying to speak. "He takes being a dog very seriously."

Aiden thought more about Mackerel, and how pleased Mack seemed when he chased a squirrel up a tree. Somehow this seemed even funnier than picturing Mackerel in a winter outfit. "There's nothing wrong with being proud of one's work," Aiden said between laughs.

Emma grabbed Aiden's arm. "I love your dog," she said when she could speak again.

Aiden gazed at Emma, suddenly serious, and said, "He loves you, too."

Emma's face was serious as well, and she let go of Aiden's arm.

They walked the rest of the way, both lost in their own thoughts.

The skating rink had just opened for the day, and it wasn't too crowded yet. Emma and Aiden rented their skates and quickly laced up. They tightened their scarves and adjusted their gloves, making sure they were as warm as possible. They were out on the ice in no time, but in silence, still in their own worlds.

They saw Alex, one of their classmates, and waved at them.

Aiden gazed at the mountain, capped in white. The nearby trees were draped in snow, some of the smallest branches sagging under the weight. It was the only landscape Aiden had ever known, yet he still found it beautiful.

"Just think, this time next year we'll be high schoolers," Emma said, ready to speak again.

Aiden, relieved to be talking, said, "I hope it won't be that much different than middle school."

"It'll be totally different!" Emma said. "Harder classes, more work . . . I can't wait!"

Aiden groaned. "It better not be a lot more work."

Emma cheerfully said, "Maybe one difference is that you'll actually like school?"

"Nah."

"It was a fun thought."

Aiden watched a group of chickadees flitting around in the snow just past the edge of the rink. "It's kinda nice that it'll be the same group of people, though, right?" he asked carefully.

"I guess so? But aren't you tired of all the same faces?"

Aiden looked hurt, and Emma said, "Not you! I love your face. I mean, I love seeing your face. You know what I mean," she finished hastily.

Aiden didn't know what she meant, not really, but he knew he shouldn't ask for clarification. He also knew he shouldn't say anything about her cheeks, which were pink with cold, and how he wondered how cold they would feel if he reached out to touch her. Emma was his best friend, and he didn't know why he was thinking about the temperature of her face.

"Just . . . wouldn't it be good to meet people we haven't known our entire lives?" Emma tried again.

Aiden still looked hurt, and Emma said, "Never mind! We'll be in college, meeting all kinds of new people, before we know it."

The reminder of college chilled Aiden more than the winter air. "Are you seriously thinking about college again?"

"Of course I am."

"You'll probably stay close to home, though, won't you?"

Emma poked Aiden with her glove and said, "Who's thinking about college now?"

"Maybe I'll take time off between high school and college."

"And do what?"

"Relax? Play music?"

"Isn't that what you do now?"

"Yeah, and I want to do more of it!"

Emma was quiet. "There's more to life outside Briar Glen, you know," she said in what she hoped was a kind voice.

"You know how it is, Emma. My family has been in Briar Glen for generations. Plus, the business—"

"I know," Emma interrupted. "But I know they love you and want what's best for you, and they'd understand if you want to leave Briar Glen. I think they'd support you no matter what you want to do. Do you think your family will just stay in Briar Glen forever? At some point, someone has to leave, right?" She tried to say all this gently, but based on the look on Aiden's face, it wasn't gentle enough.

"Well, it doesn't have to be me," Aiden said curtly. "I don't have to be the one to leave."

"I'm sorry, Aiden."

"I like living here. How do you know life would be better somewhere else?"

"I don't. That's part of the adventure."

"Your mom came back to Briar Glen after she finished college, didn't she?"

"Ten years after she finished college. In between she traveled, had new experiences—"

"But she doesn't own a local business! It's just . . . different with my family."

"Okay, okay," Emma relented.

"Sorry," Aiden said. "I guess it's a bit of a sore subject for me."

Emma changed the subject. "Did you watch the tree lighting in New York City last night?"

"Why would I do that?" He frowned. "We already had our tree lighting. Payton Daley made sure we knew her family put up the lights."

"Aiden," Emma groaned.

"What?" They both knew how magical the tree lighting in Briar Glen was, even with the family rivalry. Aiden didn't know why Emma cared so much about a tree lighting in a different city.

"You know you can go ice-skating there?" Emma asked, interrupting Aiden's thoughts. "In Rockefeller Center. Just picture it—gliding around on the ice, right in the middle of the city, with the massive tree in the background."

Emma was daydreaming, not paying attention to where she was going. She nearly bumped into Fiona Nguyen, who was holding her daughter's hand. Ms. Nguyen glanced up, steadying herself. It took her a second, but then she was able to place Emma's face.

"Sorry!" Emma said.

"It's okay," Ms. Nguyen said. "I swear the two of you were just this size." She looked down at her daughter, who was in first grade.

"First grade was pretty awesome," Emma had to admit.

Aiden frowned. "Yeah, except that's when we started getting homework."

"That's what made it so awesome!"

She and Aiden waved at Ms. Nguyen's daughter, then skated off.

"Anyway, as I was saying," Emma continued. "Rockefeller Center for ice-skating. I'm doing it someday."

"Eh, too many people," Aiden said. "It must get so crowded."

"But that's what makes it so fun!"

"Bumping into strangers and slipping on ice is your idea of fun?" Aiden asked skeptically.

"Those strangers are people with their own lives. Lives we don't know anything about. People from all over the world, all with different stories, different futures. You could be skating next to a future celebrity and not even know it!"

"I don't think I really need to know anyone else's life story."

"Aiden! People are fascinating!" Emma said enthusiastically.

Aiden wondered if Emma thought he was fascinating. He realized he was slowing down, just as Ethan Carter skated up fast behind him. "Sorry," Aiden said to Ethan as he skated away. Aiden wasn't totally sure, but he thought he was related to Ethan somehow. One of Aiden's aunts had married one of Ethan's uncles? Or was it the other way around?

"Well, I know plenty of fascinating people here in Briar Glen," Aiden said.

"There is no quota on how many fascinating people you can meet in your life."

They both looked around the rink, neither one knowing what

to say. Now they saw Lucy, Amber, and Evie, who were all just a few years older than them. They all waved at one another.

"Anyway, I do, too," Emma said.

"Do, too, what?"

"Know lots of fascinating people." Her frustration was gone, but her face was still serious.

They skated for a few moments; the only sound was their blades hitting the ice.

Emma looked around the rink again. "How many people do you recognize here?"

Aiden glanced around. "Pretty much everyone?"

"Exactly! Can you imagine going somewhere new, where no one knows you?"

The thought sent chills down Aiden's spine, and not the good kind of chills. "That sounds terrible."

Emma shook her head. "A fresh start, where no one knows about my eighth birthday party at the arcade."

"It was a fun party."

"You're missing my point!"

"A fresh start, where no one knows that you don't put marshmallows in your hot chocolate. Or where no one knows the dog who shows up at your back door."

Emma said, "But that's the thing: You meet new people, and

they learn these things about you. That's what I'm trying to say. Being somewhere where people get to learn about you, where people don't already know everything about you."

"Why do I feel like we're talking about college again?" Aiden asked. He wished he could rewind the conversation back to when they were talking about Mackerel.

Emma sighed, frustrated. "Maybe we are. I don't know."

Aiden wanted to know who Emma was talking about, who Emma wanted to meet, but just like his urge to touch her pink cheeks, the question seemed like something he should keep to himself.

He realized there were a lot of things he needed to keep to himself.

9

EMMA

Aiden slams the door shut. I want to run after him, but then what? What could I possibly say to him? I barely know what to think.

Instead, I stand in front of Sam. I'm trying to find my boyfriend, the guy who I thought I might be in love with. The guy whose glance, whose touch, could undo me. The guy who just acted jealous and then told me to chill out.

"Well, I made that awkward." Sam laughs dryly.

I don't laugh. I don't say anything.

"Would it make up for any of my behavior if I go tomorrow? Maybe? Possibly? Please?"

But I'm only half listening, still fighting the urge to run after Aiden.

"Ice-skating," he says. It seems like the decision has exhausted him. "I'm really sorry," he adds.

"For which part?" I throw my hands up in the air in exasperation. The room is filled with my neighbors, my family, people I've known my whole life. I feel a bit like I've entered some parallel dimension.

"For all of it." He reaches for my hand. "I've never told you to chill out before; I don't know why I picked tonight to say it."

"I don't either."

"I'm sorry. I guess I'm just feeling nervous about meeting your family and friends, and Aiden was so . . . so . . ."

"So *what*?"

"Nothing, never mind." He sighs. "I'm sorry about getting possessive. I know it was just an innocent kiss. I know it was just Aiden." The tingle from Sam's touch is back, but its warmth has faded. "I'm so sorry. You've never heard me say that before, and you'll never hear me say it again."

He kisses me, and the tingle tries to spread across my body, but I'm too cold.

I pull back from the kiss. "Okay. But let's not talk about it now. I just want to enjoy the party."

Sam is visibly relieved, but I'm still processing everything. And I'm still cold.

Kerry waves at me from across the room.

"What?" I mouth, but she just keeps motioning us over.

“Shall we?” Sam puts out his arm, and I hook my hand through it, dazed.

Kerry wants me to say hi to the Ramos family, who used to live in Briar Glen, and who I only sort of remember. Then I introduce them to Sam, and soon I’m introducing Sam to everyone. I try to join the conversations, I really do, but I can barely register what I’m saying, much less what anyone is saying back to me.

I mentally replay the conversation with Aiden and Sam. What I said to Aiden, telling him to come visit me, practically begging him to go ice-skating. And then the way Sam told me to chill out, how he acted about the mistletoe. What happened to his whole Emma origin story thing? And most of all, I *hated* the way Sam talked to Aiden, telling Aiden I’d never mentioned him before. It was such an awful thing for him to say. Especially because it was true. Sam didn’t know a thing about Aiden until we’d gotten to Briar Glen.

I can’t forget the way Aiden looked at me, his eyes searing into me, saying without even having to speak that I wasn’t acting like myself. I knew Easton had changed me—that being with Sam had changed me—but I thought the changes were good changes. Now I realize maybe some bad changes snuck in, too.

My mind drifts back to when I kissed Aiden’s hand. It was just an innocent kiss, but it wasn't something I'd ever done before. Then I think about Sam's possessiveness. He's next to me, his hand on the small of my back, chatting with all these new people, and I watch how easily he charms everyone I introduce him to. Because that's what he does—charms.

A terrible pit forms in my stomach as I wonder: *Has he charmed me into this relationship?*

He talks to my second-grade teacher about how one of his cousins is a teacher in Germany, but now his hand is too hot on my back, and I have to get away.

"Excuse me," I say.

Sam glances at me, then goes back to his conversation with Mr. Knight. I think I hear Sam say something about an art gallery in Bushwick just as I slip into the powder room downstairs.

I stare at myself in the mirror, one I've looked into my entire life, but the person staring back at me is someone I don't recognize.

When I emerge from the bathroom, Mr. Knight and his husband are putting on their coats, and the party seems to be winding down. My parents and sister and Sam are picking up empty plates and glasses from the dining room, and there a few party stragglers. Aiden's family left before I got a chance to talk to them.

"You okay?" Sam asks, looking concerned.

"I'm really, really tired."

Sam puts his arm around my waist. I feel like the touch sense of my body has been calibrated all wrong.

I have another restless night's sleep, Kerry snoring away. When I get downstairs the next morning, the Christmas tree lights are still on, and there are a few plates stacked by the trash can in the kitchen. Remnants of conversations from the night before float through my mind, making me cringe . . . and making me sad and angry. And very confused.

I gaze out the window into the backyard, which is blanketed in snow. It covers the old, creaky swing set that my dad installed for my fifth birthday. Every spring for the last few years we've talked about taking it down, but somehow here it still is. A cardinal hops around on one of the swings.

Did I really invite Aiden to go ice-skating with Sam and me?

Maybe Sam actually was just nervous last night? *I didn't even know he existed. Chill out.* And the way he glared at me, and at Aiden, under the mistletoe. How much grace am I willing to give him?

Then I remember how Aiden looked at me when Sam said he didn't even know Aiden existed. A mental thorn snags in my memory: Aiden never pointed out that he didn't know about Sam, either.

I'm tired and wonder if I can just go back to bed.

"Good morning," my mom says, walking into the kitchen and jolting me out of my thoughts. She yawns and makes coffee. "What do you have planned for today?"

"We're going ice-skating," I say, looking out the window again, trying to sound—and feel—cheerful.

"We?"

"Sam and me." I've never been part of a *we* before and I'm still getting used to it. "And Aiden, too."

My mom puts down the mug she just pulled from the cabinet. "Really?"

"What?" I miss being little, miss her telling me what to do, because I don't understand what is happening in my life anymore.

She studies my face. "It's just a surprising group of people to go ice-skating with, that's all."

"Surprising?" *Please, Mom, tell me what to do.*

Even if she knew my inner request, she won't be able to tell me anything, because Sam walks into the kitchen at that moment.

"Morning!" he says brightly, still in his pajamas.

"So . . . ice-skating today?" my mom asks. "Emma was just telling me."

Sam stretches and yawns. "You got it."

"Can I meet you there later?" I blurt the words out.

Sam looks baffled. "Why?"

"I want to . . . I need to spend time with Aiden."

My mom and Sam blink at me, puzzled.

"Yes." I feel more and more certain of it with each passing second. "He's my best friend, and it's my break, and I haven't seen him, not really, and I think I just need a little one-on-one time with him."

"I'm only here a few more days," Sam says. "You'll have plenty of one-on-one time then."

My mom says, "I'm going to go . . . do something" and leaves the kitchen.

"Just, like, an hour," I tell Sam. "Then you can join us. Okay?"

He sighs. "If you want to spend time with your friend, I'm not going to stop you. I mean, I wouldn't stop you, of course."

"Of course. He's my friend—has been my friend since we were little kids. I know you respect that, right?"

But it's like he hasn't heard me. "You know, I think this is actually a good idea. I can get started on the outline for Dr. Caldwell."

"Thank you for understanding." It's not quite the support I was hoping for, and I want to push it more. But my need to see Aiden as soon as possible is stronger, so I let it go. Or try to.

After breakfast, I walk to the rink quickly. Well, as quickly as I can on the narrow sidewalk. As I get closer, I hear laughter and shouts of glee, and then I round the corner, and I'm at the rink.

I collect my skates, put them on, and check my phone: 10:53. I text Aiden: *I'm here.*

I put my phone down, and he's walking toward me, holding a pair of skates. I feel my face light up, and I can almost pretend this is like any other time we've gone ice-skating. Like it hasn't been almost a year since we've done this.

He's surprised to see me.

"I know, I'm early!" I say. "I swear that Easton has made me more on time for things."

"You're here."

"Yes. Early!"

"But you're here. Not *we're* here."

"Huh?"

"I guess I wasn't sure if I was expecting Sam to be here or not."

"Oh, he's going to come later."

"Why?"

"I told him I wanted to spend time with just you."

Aiden's cheeks color. "Why would you want to do that?"

"Because I don't think the last few times we've seen each other have exactly been quality hangout time. Unless you think so, and that's the kind of friendship you want now?" I can't believe how calm I keep my voice.

"Emma! You're joking, right? Of course I don't want that."

"Just making sure." Relief surges through my body.

"I'd never want that." He flushes more.

"Okay."

"Okay."

We eye each other awkwardly for a few seconds.

"Anyway," I say, clearing my throat. "Want to put those on?" I nod at his feet, and he slips his skates on.

Soon we're gliding on the ice. I stare at the mountain off in the distance. Another thing I don't think I've realized how much I miss. I see more familiar faces, including people from last night, like Mr. Knight and his family.

We all wave at one another, and a second later, Darby, a girl a few years younger than Aiden and me, glides by, saying, "Hi!" and then "Bye!"

"I guess Briar Glen is a pretty small town," Aiden says.

"Really small."

"Is it weird being back?"

"Weird doesn't even come close to describing it."

Aiden waits for me to say more, like he always does.

"Everything is so recognizable, like Briar Glen looks the same, but everyone just seems slightly different somehow."

"Well . . . it *has* been six months."

"Six months," I repeat. "When I started at Easton it was summer, and the humidity was like nothing in Briar Glen. Oppressive. Inescapable. Then it was fall, and it was beautiful, but it wasn't Briar Glen. And then winter. Or almost winter. I don't know. December. But now I'm here. The seasons passed so quickly, and everything happens so fast there, and I feel like I can never catch my breath. It's kind of hard sometimes."

I'm not sure if I'm making sense. I tried to tell Sam once that everything seemed to happen so fast at Easton, but he just told me that's how New York is. I knew it was more complicated than that, but I didn't know how to explain it. And now, as I look at Aiden I see it: He understands me. Even if I don't understand myself.

"You could have told me all of that, you know."

"I know. I could have told you a lot of things."

"Why didn't you?"

"I don't know," I say honestly. "I guess I didn't know where to begin."

"Did . . . friends at Easton help you adjust?"

"My roommate, Victoria, did. She's been at Easton since her freshman year and knows everyone. She's how I met Sam."

Aiden flinches, then says, "So Sam helped you get used to Easton, too?"

"Yeah. He loves school, like I do. He grew up in the city and showed me around. And now I get to show him around Briar Glen!"

"You both like school," Aiden says, though it seems more like he's talking to himself than to me. And then, in a louder voice, "You started dating him pretty much right after you moved to Easton?"

I feel myself bristle a little at the question. "Yeah, I guess so. Why are you asking?"

"I was just wondering. Sam sure is . . . a character."

"I know. Last night was horrible. Will you please try to forgive him?" I should tell Aiden that I'm still trying to forgive Sam myself.

"He told you to chill out! Doesn't he know that's in the top five things to never say to you?"

"If he didn't, he does now." I think more about last night. "That's the first time he's ever said anything like that before. I think he's nervous about meeting everyone. Especially you."

"Why? He said himself that he didn't even know I existed."

I hear the hurt in his voice. "I didn't tell you about him, either," I offer, but the hurt stays on Aiden's face.

I sigh. "I just didn't know what to say about you."

"Wow, thanks," Aiden says, the hurt deepening.

"Not in a bad way."

"There's a good way?"

"No, listen, Aiden. You're my best friend. I knew I'd miss you, but once I got to Easton, I *really* missed you, and I knew if I talked about you I'd miss you even more." I miss him now too, though he's right next to me.

"You missed me?" Aiden says in a soft voice.

"Of course I did. I hope you missed me!" It slips out of my mouth.

"Obviously," Aiden says in the same soft voice. He's skating next to me, head down.

"Sam is only here a few more days." I feel the need to keep talking. "He's leaving the day after the winter festival to go to a ski resort with his family."

"Ski resort." Aiden whistles. "Fancy."

"I'm still not sure how I feel about him participating in the race," I admit.

"Oh yeah?"

"It seems like it should only be for Briar Glen residents. It's bringing together these two different parts of my life."

"But isn't that why Sam is here? To meet your family and get to know this part of your life?" He says it with a weariness to his voice.

"Yeah, it is. It's just confusing sometimes." It feels even more confusing standing next to Aiden, telling him all this.

Aiden is quiet again. He takes a deep breath and says, "Does he make you happy?"

"Yes," I answer automatically.

"Well, that's all that matters, then, isn't it?"

"You sound like my mom! But no, I don't think it is. I think there's a lot more to it."

Aiden looks at me questioningly.

"It made more sense when I said it in my head," I say. "Can you please at least try to give him a chance? Please?" I think I'm asking myself the same thing too: to give Sam another chance.

I look into Aiden's eyes, the golden flecks almost dancing. "Okay," he says.

I put my hand on his shoulder, relieved. "Thank you."

He glances at my hand, and I put it back at my side. "Aiden, another thing I should have already said . . . I'm sorry for leaving like I did. I hated it. I still do."

"I hated it, too. Why did you do it, Emma? Why did you leave without saying goodbye? And in June! I didn't even know you were gone until Jo told me."

Suddenly, it's as if I can feel all the pain he's felt in the last six months—all the pain I caused—on top of my own. He didn't deserve this. Neither of us did.

"I"—I struggle to find the right words to say—"I guess I did it because . . ."

But I don't get the chance to finish my sentence because Sam appears in the distance, carrying two steaming cups from Cup o' Jo.

10

AIDEN

"He's already here?" I ask Emma.

She checks her phone. "He's early," she says, but smiles and waves at him.

Sam is waving at Emma—at us?—to come over, so Emma and I skate off the ice.

"I thought you guys might be cold, so I picked up some hot chocolate for you."

"What kind?" I ask, and Emma shoots me a look. "I mean, thank you."

Sam hands us the cups. "Did I get it right?" he asks eagerly.

"Peppermint hot chocolate, extra hot," Emma says after taking a sip. "Thank you."

"I know it's your favorite," Sam says, pecking her on the cheek. "How is your drink, Aiden?"

Part of me wonders if I should have him try it first,

make sure it isn't poisoned, but I take a cautious sip.

Regular hot chocolate, no peppermint. And marshmallows.

He did this on purpose—I just know it—but I'm not giving him the satisfaction of calling him out. "Yeah, thanks," I say, looking at Sam with fake gratitude. "It's perfect."

"Perfect." There's that wink again. "I know I'm early," he continues, "but you guys can drink your hot chocolate and warm up. I'm going to do a few practice laps, and then I'll see you out there?"

"Oh, sure," Emma says. She sits next to Sam while he laces up his skates, and I sit down on a bench across from her. She hasn't taken another sip of her hot chocolate.

Sam stands up, rolls his shoulders, and gives Emma a kiss on the forehead. "See you in a minute."

"See you soon!" I say with too much enthusiasm.

Sam gives me a quick, suspicious glance, then skates off.

"Well, he sure is prompt," I scoff.

"Aiden . . ."

"Just an observation!"

"I know this must be strange," she says, stating the obvious. "I don't expect you guys to be best friends, but can you at least try to be nice to him?"

"Maybe he should try being nice to *me*." I realize I sound like a five-year-old, so I take a breath. "I promise I'll be nicer to him. Scout's honor."

"You were never a scout," Emma says, but she's smiling. "How do I know I can trust you?" She takes a sip of her drink and then stands up to throw the cup in the trash.

I stand up, too, and toss my cup in the trash can as well. "We've known each other since we were five; we have hung out probably a million times, maybe more; we've been in school together since kindergarten; and when have I ever let you down before?" I say the last part quickly, then catch myself. "Well, I hope I haven't let you down."

Emma studies her skates, then looks up at me. "You've never let me down," she says quietly.

"Oh?" I say, in a quiet voice as well.

"I don't think missing someone counts as letting them down, does it?" Her eyes are on mine. "I missed you."

I take a step toward her, but I forget I'm on skates, and I stumble, Emma catching me.

My hands are on her shoulders, and it's just like the night before, and I can't believe I've forgotten what being close to the warmth of her body feels like. How can I forget something that feels both comfortable . . . and filled with sparks? Neither of us says anything as we look into each other's eyes. Her eyes. I have missed her eyes.

"I'm sorry," I say in a low voice.

"I already told you that you didn't let me down," she says in practically a whisper.

"I should have texted more. Like real texts, not just pictures of random things. I should have called. Sent a carrier pigeon. Anything. More than I did," I say. "I missed you. So much." It feels like a relief to finally get the words out, to finally unburden my heart.

Emma shakes her head. "No, I should have. I'm the one with access to pigeons!"

We both laugh, and we're standing so close that I feel the puff of air from her laugh on my cheek.

I hear the *clomp, clomp* of skates on the ground, and Sam stands behind Emma. He's not happy. I pull away, and Emma turns and says, "Sam!"

"My skate slipped," I say weakly, as a form of apology. But why am I apologizing to Sam?

"Are you going to skate or not?" he asks Emma, and now he's the one who sounds like a five-year-old.

"I'm ready!" Emma says, like the moment with me never happened.

Was it a moment with me?

She glides onto the ice, but Sam gives me a final glare before skating onto the ice himself, ahead of Emma.

I think of Emma's words. *You've never let me down. I missed you.*

I want to ask her how she missed me, what she missed about me. Did she miss me in the same way that I missed her? That sometimes it was hard to breathe I missed her so much? The ache in my chest waking me up every morning? Surely, that can't be the kind of missing she's talking about. We're friends. Or were friends. She missed my friendship. I shake my head, trying to unscramble it.

I agreed to try to be nicer to Sam. I've known Emma for more than ten years. No matter what he says, I will not let Sam win. Especially in my town.

I breathe deeply and skate onto the ice. Emma and I only got off the ice a few moments ago, but it doesn't feel as smooth now.

I join Emma. "There you are!" Her cheeks are flushed with cold. It makes her looks so innocent. "I was just thinking that ice-skating at Rockefeller Center was incredible, but I might like this better?"

"Really?" I say, surprised.

"Really," she says back. "I think it's one of those things I romanticized, you know? Something I had dreamed about. But I realized maybe it was better left there, in my dreams."

"Maybe you just weren't skating with the right person," I say.

Emma's eyes widen, and Sam skates over now, too, making a

big show of stopping next to us and spraying ice everywhere, including all over me.

"Sorry! Bad habit!" He skates away, then comes right back, spraying more ice, this time on Emma.

Sam laughs, and Emma rolls her eyes as she brushes herself off.

"Did he do this at Rockefeller Center?" I ask Emma, refusing to wipe away the ice.

Emma won't meet my eye. "It was kind of funny."

I'm failing to see any humor. "Which part?"

"You'd have to be there," Sam says.

"I'm here now. Hilarious."

"I'm freezing!" Sam complains. "Let's keep moving."

"Good idea," Emma says.

But I don't move. I just watch them skate away, ice still dripping off me.

Sam puts out his arm to Emma, but she doesn't take it.

They make a whole lap, and then I eventually join in, skating behind them. Sam puts out his arm again, and this time Emma takes it, but just the tips of her gloves are touching his arm. They aren't talking to each other, just skating.

You've never let me down. I missed you. The words are running around in a loop in my head.

Emma skates back to me. "Will you join us, please?"

She doesn't realize the effect her eyes have on me. Or maybe she does, because I follow her. The three of us make a line, with Emma in the middle.

I have to look over her to see Sam, and it's awkward, but I think about Emma's ask—that I give him a chance.

Sam leans forward, seemingly unbothered by the awkwardness of how we're positioned. "Emma was just telling me you play guitar?"

It's ironic that he didn't even know I existed and now suddenly he knows what I like to do, but I say, "Yeah. I started when I was ten."

"That's cool. How often do you have lessons?"

"I don't take lessons. I just kind of learned on my own."

I think I see Sam roll his eyes.

"What kind of songs do you play?"

"Mostly old stuff. Some punk, I guess. Stuff my parents used to listen to."

"You should hear him play 'Last Night on Earth,'" Emma chimes in.

Sam gives us a blank stare, and Emma says, "It's an old Green Day song."

Sam nods, thinking. "Is that the song that Arabella is always playing?"

"She's who I told you about," Emma explains to me.

"She's been taking lessons since she was six," Sam adds.

Emma frowns. "Lessons are just one way to learn."

Sam scoffs. "Obviously, they worked; you've heard how good she is!"

"I guess so," Emma says.

"Anyway," Sam continues, "I can play piano."

"But I thought you stopped taking lessons when you were younger?" Emma asks.

"I haven't forgotten how to play." He puts his hands out in front of him, an invisible keyboard, and he looks so cheesy that I can't hide my laugh.

"Something you'd like to share with the class, Aiden?" Sam says, putting his arms down.

"Nope. You do know that Emma used to take piano lessons, right?"

"She stopped in fourth grade," he says smugly. "We should play together sometime, Emma."

"Where?" she asks.

"At Easton. In the music room."

"That's only for students who currently play an instrument."

Sam winks. "I'm sure they can bend the rules for us."

"Why?" Emma and I say at the same time.

Sam turns red. "Because I'm sure they can. It's no big deal."

He shrugs, and that's when I realize, when it really sinks in, that he's spent his life getting what he wants.

"Must be nice," I say, and I just know I'm going to regret it.

Sam swerves on the ice and stops in front of me, blocking my path. "What's *that* supposed to mean?"

I want to tell him exactly what I mean—that he's a privileged jerk who thinks he can impress people with his money and status, who thinks he can charm his way into anything. But I look at Emma and think better of it.

Give him a chance.

"Nothing," I finally say. "Nothing at all."

"I think I need some water," Emma says, eyeing Sam. "Anyone else need anything?"

I shake my head, and Sam says, "Do you want me to get it?"

"No, I need a break," Emma says before skating off the ice and disappearing around the corner to the concession stand.

Sam and I stand on the ice in an awkward silence. I concentrate on the mountain, looking anywhere but at Sam.

"I think I need a little break, too," he admits. "No offense."

"That's a good idea," I agree, relieved.

I watch his retreating figure, and I stand at the side of the rink, debating if I should just leave.

Give him a chance. You've never let me down. I missed you.

I keep staring at the mountain. I wonder how many ice-skaters it's watched. I wonder how many people it's seen falling in love, falling out of love.

I'm not hanging on to the rail when it happens: I feel a thud against my back, and I'm tipping forward, the ice meeting the side of my face—hard.

The ice is so cold, but my cheek feels like it's on fire.

I hear an "Oh, man, are you okay?" I blink, and I see a pair of skates inches away from my face. I sit up, dizzy, and Sam is staring at me, hand over his mouth in shock. "Are you all right?"

"I—I don't know what happened." I push myself up so I'm leaning against the rink wall. "I was standing here, and then I fell over," I say, trying to get my bearings.

"I'm *so* sorry!" Sam says apologetically. "I was skating so fast—I'm not used to these rinks with so much open space—I didn't realize how fast I was going, and I crashed into you!"

I almost believe him . . . until I see his smirk. And that says it all.

"You did it on purpose!" I shout.

"Me?" Sam feigns innocence. "I would never."

"Liar!" I'm not falling for it—ever—and he knows it.

"Listen," he says more quietly when passersby turn in our direction, concerned. He puts an arm around my neck and brings my face closer to his, like we're good buddies. "I know you and Emma have this past. But it's from when you were kids. It's history."

"Yeah, well, that history isn't going to disappear."

He takes his arm off me, then examines my face with that pompous smirk. "Like I said, Emma never mentioned you—so I know you don't mean all that much to her. Thank goodness she moved out of Briar Glen and found me; you're certainly not good enough for her."

I blink, in such shock that I'm unable to make a sound. I don't even know where to start to defend my friend or myself.

"What did you just say?" I finally manage.

"Too fast for you, country boy?" Sam mocks. "Let me make it clear so even you can understand: You. Are. Not. Good. Enough. For. Emm—" But he stops himself, and a horrified look washes over his face.

Because Emma suddenly appears, and she's heard everything.

DECEMBER, TWO YEARS AGO.

Aiden put down his guitar triumphantly. Without his music, the room was much quieter. He heard a scratching at his door and opened it to find Mack standing there, looking relieved for the silence in his room.

"Sorry, bud," Aiden said, petting his dog.

Mackerel looked longingly downstairs, and Aiden heard voices. He listened for a second.

Emma! he thought.

Mackerel bounded down the stairs, and Aiden followed, just as he heard his grandma saying, "And that was the last time I ate any kind of shellfish. Covered in hives from head to toe. Even my hives had hives!"

Mackerel ran to the living room, where Aiden's grandma and Emma were. Mack sat on Emma's feet and looked up at Aiden, tail thumping.

Emma petted Mack's head and said, "And you never got any kind of allergy testing?"

"Pshaw! For what!" Aiden's grandma said. "I already found out the hard way to stay away from certain kinds of fish."

"What are you guys talking about?" Aiden asked curiously, though he wasn't totally sure he wanted the answer.

"Why we don't do the Feast of the Seven Fishes at our house," his grandma said. "I was telling Emma about my allergy. Had clams for the first time and the last time when I was four. Boy, you should have seen the hives!" She chuckled. "Glad the allergy didn't come out the other way, if you know what I mean!"

"Grandma!" Aiden said.

He shot a glance at Emma, but she was laughing.

"What's the matter?" his grandma said. "Everyone—"

"Grandma!" Aiden said again, his cheeks coloring this time.

"I'm the one who asked!" Emma laughed. "A lot of Italian American families celebrate the Feast of the Seven Fishes on Christmas Eve."

Aiden groaned. "Aren't you happy you asked?"

Emma just laughed again, though, and absent-mindedly petted Mack's head. After a moment she said, "You know, shellfish aren't actually fish, but seafood. So you could do the feast and just not eat any shellfish?"

Aiden's grandma snorted. "If it lives in the water, it's a fish as far as I'm concerned!" She nodded, satisfied with herself.

"So the reason we don't do the feast is because Grandma doesn't like fish," Aiden joked.

His grandma put up her hand. "Ah! Do I need to tell the story again? When I was four—"

"Got it, Grandma!" Aiden hastily interjected. Then, to Emma, "Should we head out? The festival started, right?"

"Sure!" Emma stood up and gave Mackerel another pat on the head.

Aiden's grandma huffed and picked up her cup of coffee. "Don't go breaking any necks out there."

"We won't!" they replied in unison, Mack trailing behind them.

"Your grandma is so funny," Emma said in the mudroom as Aiden pulled on his winter boots.

Aiden put on his coat. "She's so . . . something."

Mackerel looked up at them hopefully.

"I'm sorry, Mack, no dogs allowed at the race," Aiden said, scratching behind his dog's ears.

"Your grandpa should make a sled for Mack."

The dog jumped up on his hind legs and knocked Emma off her feet, then climbed into her lap. Emma giggled from the floor as Mack lapped his giant tongue across her face.

"Mackerel! Where are your manners?" Aiden asked, crouching down, trying to stop laughing. But then the dog wiggled over to him and knocked him over, too, and then Aiden was on the floor next to Emma, having his face vigorously cleaned by his dog.

"Mack!" Aiden squealed, trying to gently push his dog away, but Mackerel was on a mission, and his tail just thumped harder the more Emma and Aiden laughed.

Finally, Aiden was able to move Mack's head away from his face, and the dog seemed proud of himself.

Aiden sat up, but Emma was practically in hysterics next to him. Mackerel sneezed a huge, wet sneeze, right onto Emma—who yelped and laughed even harder—and then trotted away.

Emma sat up, wiping her face.

"He only sneezes on people he really loves," Aiden said, somewhat apologetically as he stood.

The word *love* hung in the air. Aiden and Emma both knew that Aiden was talking about Mackerel, but it still seemed like an odd word to exist between the two of them. And it made Emma stop laughing.

She stood and moved closer to him. Then she put out her hand, and Aiden didn't know what was happening, or was about to happen. Her hand got closer and closer to his face. She used her hand to measure her height next to Aiden.

"I still can't believe we're exactly the same height!" Emma said, standing very close to Aiden.

Emma could smell toothpaste on Aiden's breath, and Aiden could smell the coconut in Emma's hair. They blinked at each other, looking directly into each other's eyes.

Emma was the first to step back. "We should probably go . . ."

"You're right," Aiden said, forcing himself out of his temporary trance.

He zipped up his coat and put on his hat, and soon they were out the door. They stopped by Aiden's garage to grab their sleds. Aiden's grandpa had customized sleds for them. He even engraved their initials in the corners of the sleds. Aiden and Emma looked around the garage, at his grandpa's workbench. It was full of projects in various states of progress. There were cutting boards, parts of a table, sled Christmas ornaments, and of course real, usable sleds.

Emma admired one of the sleds in progress. "It's not quite the same. But I was reading the other day about sleigh riding in Norway. I kind of want to study abroad in Norway. There's a place where actual reindeer pull a sleigh. But it isn't a competition. It'd be fun to do someday, though, wouldn't it?" Emma stared off into the distance, thinking about traveling through the Nordic wilderness on a sleigh being pulled by reindeer.

"Sure, yeah, maybe, someday," Aiden said. "But today, right now, we should go to the winter festival in Briar Glen." He started to pull Emma's sled out of the garage by its rope, just as Emma reached for it, too, and their hands touched. They were both wearing gloves, but both could feel the contact run through their entire bodies.

"Oh, sorry," Aiden said, letting go of the rope, not looking at Emma.

"For what? Getting my sled out for me?" Emma teased.

Aiden looked back at her again, and his cheeks were a little red. The hazel in his eyes seemed brighter against the white snow.

"We should go," Emma said, forcing herself to look away from Aiden.

They were quiet on the walk to the park, pulling their sleds behind them.

The park was busy, with all kinds of food and drinks tents. Including, of course, the Cup o' Jo tent, which is where Aiden and Emma stopped first. The line was long, as always, but moved quickly, and soon it was their turn.

"Good day for a winter festival, isn't it?" Jo asked, rubbing her hands together. Her cheeks were rosy with cold, and excitement. The winter festival was one of her favorite days of the year. "Your usual peppermint hot chocolates?"

"Yes, please," Emma said.

"You guys ready for the race?" Jo asked, peering at their sleds.

"Born ready," Emma said.

Aiden nodded, distracted.

Jo handed Aiden and Emma their peppermint hot chocolates. "Lucy and Amber are already out there somewhere."

Aiden faced the crowd. "Are there more people here this year than usual?"

"Probably?" Jo said. "We seem to have more competitors every year!"

Aiden sipped his hot chocolate, grateful for the comfortable warmth.

Emma took a sip of her hot chocolate. "Shall we?"

Aiden nodded again.

Jo said, "Enjoy!" and Emma and Aiden were on their way.

They checked the schedule posted to one of the utility poles. "We have another thirty minutes until the race for teen sledders," Emma said.

Aiden contemplated the sledding hill. "Did the hill get bigger this year?" he asked.

Emma observed the hill. "There might be more snow up there than last year, but it shouldn't be a huge difference."

She looked at her friend carefully. "You okay? What's up?"

Aiden shook his head, trying to shake the weird sense of doom that was suddenly snaking its way through his body.

Emma studied her friend, not convinced that he was okay, but not wanting to push it, either. "How about we build a snowman?"

"A snowman?" Aiden echoed.

"Yes!" Emma said decisively. "This way."

She found an empty snowy patch on the field. They parked their sleds and rested their hot chocolates on top of the sleds.

The snow was a little icy: perfect for building a snowman. Emma and Aiden pushed a huge mound of snow into a giant ball for the snowman's body.

They sat back on their heels, admiring their work. Emma shaped the ball with her hands, smoothing out the lumps and bumps. "What do you think?" she asked.

"Not bad," Aiden said.

They set to work making the second part of the snowman's body, its middle, rolling and packing snow, and then lifting it onto the other ball of snow.

"We need really good eyes," Emma said contemplatively. "Hmm . . . acorns?"

While she looked around, Aiden pushed a mound of snow into a ball for the snowman's head.

They were both so busy that they didn't see Jason, Dustin, and Graham approaching.

"Look who it is," Graham said with a cruel cackle. "Aiden and his girlfriend."

The three boys stood next to the snowman. Aiden tried to think of something to say, but Emma spoke first. "You must be here to help us build a snowman!" She said it with such enthusiasm that it was hard for Aiden to tell if she was being sarcastic or genuine.

It didn't matter, though, because the boys laughed liked they'd never heard anything so funny. Aiden was still trying to think of what to say, but Emma just stared at them until they stopped laughing.

"What are you looking at?" Jason snapped.

"My parents always told me that if I couldn't say anything nice, I shouldn't say anything at all," Emma said sweetly.

"Ooooh," Dustin said, as Graham added, "She got you!"

Aiden tried to hide his smile, but not fast enough. "What are you laughing at?" Jason snapped.

"Remember what I just said about not saying anything nice?" Emma scoffed. "Now, if you'll excuse me, I have a snowman to build."

Dustin and Graham laughed again, and Jason's face was beet red. Jason glared at Aiden. "What's it like, having to have your *girlfriend* defend you?"

Hearing the word a second time, now it was Aiden's turn to blush. "She's not my girlfriend," he said quietly, not looking at anyone.

"What's that? Didn't hear you," Jason said, crossing his arms.

"She's not my girlfriend!" he said in a louder voice, this time making eye contact with Emma.

She held his gaze, and something fluttered around near their hearts.

"Please! You two should just get married," Graham chimed in.

Emma and Aiden still watched each other. The distance between them seemed much smaller. They didn't realize their snowman had been knocked over until they heard Graham, Jason, and Dustin whooping.

Emma tore her eyes away from Aiden's. She glared at the three boys, but they were already walking away. She was breathing hard, and she had that knot in her chest that meant she was about to cry.

Aiden was once again at a loss for words. Emma took shallow breaths, and he wanted to hug her, but he didn't want the other guys to come back and start teasing them again. "They're jerks," he said, but the words felt weak.

Emma sniffled and wiped her nose on her mittens. "I'm not going to comment," she said. "Can't say anything nice, right?"

Aiden wanted to protest, wanted Emma to say something mean about them, but she didn't. So he didn't, either.

Their eyes locked again, and they didn't look away from each other until the megaphone crackled to life, and Frank Kerne, a city council member said, "Sledders, make your way over to the hill! Kids, ages six to ten, head to your starting point halfway up the hill."

Emma jumped, and Aiden was startled.

Emma had wanted to build a snowman to try to distract Aiden from whatever was bugging him, but now she worried she had just made things worse. Aiden hated that Emma was so upset.

"It's not really a great day for making a snowman," Aiden said, standing up.

"I guess not. I'm sorry . . ." Emma trailed off, not sure what she was apologizing for. Their classmates' cruelty? That wasn't her fault. That people thought Aiden and Emma were boyfriend and girlfriend? She felt her cheeks coloring.

"You didn't do anything wrong."

"I know."

They stared at each other again, but Mr. Kerne was back on the megaphone, so Emma and Aiden trudged through the snow, pulling their sleds, neither of them knowing what to say.

They heard the hoots and shouts of the kids sledding down the hill, their faces and snowsuits a blur of color.

The megaphone squealed, and Mr. Kerne named each child as they landed at the base of the hill. There was Margo, who Emma used to babysit for; Nova, who lived just a few doors down from Aiden.

Neither Aiden nor Emma spoke until they got to the base of the hill, where they stopped. They gazed at each other, until Emma said, "You ready?"

"Yep!" Aiden said, hoping he sounded enthusiastic.

But they both just stood there for a moment, Aiden with an odd sense of dread, and Emma with an odd sense of . . . something.

Other sledders started to pass them, including Jason, who bumped against Aiden, causing Aiden to lose his balance for a second.

"Let's go," Emma said, glaring at Jason.

She and Aiden pulled their sleds up the hill, which was a little more slippery under the icy snow. Aiden felt his hands sweating inside his gloves. He didn't know why he was feeling weird—he'd raced since he was six years old.

They reached the top of the hill and put their sleds down carefully. They were at the very edge of the group, right next to the rope that indicated where the racing area ended. Emma smiled at Aiden, but his complexion looked off somehow.

"You sure you're okay?" she asked again.

He wasn't, but he also didn't know how to explain the sense of dread and doom that was consuming his body.

The megaphone squealed, Mr. Kerne saying the race would begin in one minute, but Emma and Aiden still stood facing each other. "Jeez, why do I feel like we're going away on some long vacation or something? I'll see you in, like, one minute!" Emma said.

Aiden had the same sensation, that they were departing on expeditions, both of them heading off in different directions, which just made his unsettled feeling further bloom. "Yeah, see you soon," he said distractedly.

"Racers, on the count of five!" Mr. Kerne yelled. He counted down, and the spectators joined, and then Emma and Aiden sat on their sleds. They pushed off with a gentle whoosh.

Emma started laughing, and Aiden felt himself smiling. How did he always forget how fun this was? But something still felt wrong. They raced faster and faster down the hill, their sleds rapidly picking up speed. Aiden heard everyone around him laughing, shouting, but it seemed to be coming to him from some great distance. He was still trying to figure out why everything seemed so far away when he realized he was veering off to the side, getting closer to the rope. He steered his sled away, but the racer in front of him was going slower than he was, so Aiden got close to the rope again, then too close, and the rope got tangled up in Aiden's arms, knocking him off his sled. He watched his sled continue down the hill, riderless.

His sled kept going faster and faster now that its load had been lifted, and Aiden watched in horror as the sled bumped into Emma. She turned, confused, but the sled kept zipping past her and down the hill, where it landed at the bottom.

Mr. Kerne laughed as he said, "And here comes a Gallo sled, without its Gallo rider!"

Aiden tried to laugh—everything was fine—but then he saw his left arm, which was twisted around the rope at an angle that looked all wrong—and, he realized, *felt* all wrong.

Emma stood up and grabbed her sled. Her cheeks were pink, and her hat was askew, and she was grinning from ear to ear. Until she saw Aiden. Then she dropped her sled and ran up the hill.

"What happened?" Her face was losing its color.

"I don't know," Aiden said. "I somehow got off course." He shrugged, but the motion hurt. "Ow," he said softly.

He glanced at his arm, then looked away again, feeling slightly nauseated. Mr. Kerne was talking over the megaphone, but his words were jumbled.

Emma sat down in the snow next to him, and a second later an EMT in a fluorescent vest traipsed up the hill. "What hurts?" she asked in a bored voice.

"My arm."

The EMT gingerly touched Aiden's tangled-up arm, and Aiden was surprised it didn't hurt more.

Emma's color was returning. "That looked really bad."

"It isn't?" Aiden still wasn't able to look at his arm as the EMT gently moved it.

Emma watched the EMT working.

"Emma?" Aiden said.

She snapped her attention back to Aiden. "No, I don't think so."

Aiden's mom climbed up the hill now, a panicked expression on her face. Just before she reached them, the EMT said, "There."

Aiden cautiously checked, and his arm was free.

"Is it broken?" Aiden's mom asked. "Are you okay?"

"No, likely just a sprain. But you can take him to a physician if you'd like," the EMT said, standing up.

"Oh, thank goodness," Aiden's mom said.

"How did you even end up over here?" Emma asked.

Aiden looked at his arm, which didn't seem to be part of his body.

"I thought my sled was going to hit you."

Emma was confused.

"After I fell off. I thought my sled would bump into you and you'd fall off and get hurt."

Emma was still confused. "How would I get hurt?"

"If someone else bumped into you. I don't know, actually." It made less sense the more Aiden thought about it.

"I'm so glad you're okay," Aiden's mom said, reaching out to hug her son carefully. "Do you think we should take you to the doctor, though? Just to be on the safe side?"

Aiden wiggled his wrist. It did feel a little funny. "Maybe."

"Why don't you see how you feel standing up?" Aiden's mom suggested.

She helped Aiden to his feet, and the crowd of spectators erupted in applause. Aiden had forgotten about all of Briar Glen being at the bottom of the hill. And now all of Briar Glen knew he couldn't even ride a sled. A sled his grandfather had built just for him. The embarrassment and shame hurt much more than his wrist.

Emma grinned. "What a relief! I guess no guitar playing for a few days." But she could see the pure mortification on Aiden's face.

"No guitar playing for a few days. And no sled racing ever again!" He walked down the rest of the hill as quickly as he could, but the descent felt agonizingly slow, embarrassment more and more painful with each and every step.

11

EMMA

"Emms!" Sam says sweetly when he realizes I'm standing there. "I was telling Aiden here that I'm not used to going so fast on my skates, and I accidentally bumped into him when I tried to stop."

"He's lying," Aiden says. "He did it on purpose. And you heard what he said, right? That I'm not good enough for you." He sounds desperate. "I've been trying, Emma." He pushes himself up. "I've been trying so hard to be nice to him, but I can't do it anymore."

I look back and forth between Sam and Aiden, speechless. I know what I saw. And what I heard.

"Just . . . leave me alone," Aiden says, skating away.

"Aiden, wait!" I say, but he's moving away from me too fast.

He pushes past Elena, past Colby, former classmates; past Lucy and Jack, who are skating with their arms linked. They all watch him curiously, but he doesn't stop.

I turn back to Sam, who is toeing at the ice with his skate. He looks up at me sheepishly. "He'll be fine," he says. "Just give him some time to cool off."

"How . . . how *could* you?" I say, with anger that surprises even me.

"I already *told* you," he says in a small voice. "It was an accident."

Liar.

"Which part? When you pushed over my best friend? Or when you said he wasn't good enough for me?"

"Please, Emma . . ." I know it's a last-ditch effort to get me to believe him, but even he knows I'm not buying this little ruse. "You know it's true. He's not good enough for you. He's your childhood best friend. He'll never change. That's why he's part of your past. I get to be part of your future." He gently tips my head toward him. His touch used to feel like my favorite touch in the world. Warm and soft and all mine.

But not now.

I pull my head away, look around at all the familiar faces, some of which are turned in our direction. Faces I've known my whole life. Not like the person who is standing in front of me, who is now a stranger. I stare at Sam, and for the first time, I see the real him. The charmer, the snob, the liar. The real Sam. And I don't like him one bit.

"No. You don't get to decide my future," I say. "No one does but me."

"Emma," he says, with a sternness in his voice that I've never heard before. "I can understand what it's like be home after all this time." He looks around the rink, more people watching us now. He speaks more quietly. "Remember? We talked about it. But don't let that confuse you or stand in the way of your goals. Think about your potential college opportunities you have going to Easton. An Ivy League school, medical school, anything you want!"

"I never said anything about not going back to Easton. It's the middle of the school year! Of course I'm going back."

"Phew!" Sam says. "Thought I lost you for a minute there!" He starts to lift my face, but I pull away again.

"You did."

Sam opens and closes his mouth a few times, then laughs nervously. "Did what?"

"Lose me," I clarify. "I need to go."

"That's a good idea," Sam says, stepping toward me. "It's been such a busy few days. We should rest. Maybe work on that outline."

I step away from him. "No. *We* don't need to do anything. But *I* need to leave."

"You . . . you can't be serious!" There is that real Sam again, anger and shock twisting his features. "Are you breaking up with me over some small-town loser you're not even friends with?"

I hear gasps as Sam's voice echoes across the ice. Lucy and Jack have stopped skating and are watching the scene now, too.

"No," I say. "I'm breaking up with you because you're arrogant and self-centered and mean. I let myself get too wrapped up in you, or the idea of you, and I started to lose myself, too. But now I've seen who you really are, and you're not even a quarter of the person Aiden is!"

I hear more gasps, and now it seems like the entire rink is watching and listening.

Sam looks around now. "Briar Glen is beautiful!" he says weakly. "You're all lucky to live here!"

No one says anything back, including me.

"Emma . . ." Sam says, in a quieter voice. I think his eyes might actually be watering, too. "My stuff is at your house, and I'm supposed to stay longer, and—and . . . you can't just leave me here!"

"Oh yes I can," I say. And I do exactly that.

I turn and skate off the ice, and Sam is still standing there—that new, raw expression on his face of someone not getting what they want, when they've gotten what they wanted for their entire lives.

People start skating again, but Sam just stands there, in his sea of strangers.

I take off my skates, and I think I hear voices I recognize saying things like, "What a jerk!" and "Poor Aiden." and "Emma went to boarding school?" But everything has become one giant blur of sound and movement.

In a daze, I wander toward the Briar Glen town square. I'm not sure why I'm going there, but I'm not sure of much right now. I think I just broke up with my first boyfriend, and I think my best friend might hate me.

Leave me alone.

Aiden was trying so hard. He tried to like my boyfriend. My boyfriend, who ended up hurting Aiden, and ended up being someone I didn't even recognize. The longer I walk, the deeper my sense of shame gets. Will Aiden ever forgive me? How can I ever even attempt to apologize to him?

My phone buzzes in my pocket. It's a text from Sam, but I don't bother to read the message before I turn off my phone. I look at the lights on all the poles along my walk.

Aiden.

It's one of those cold, sunless December days, and the tree in the square is already lit, the lights around the gazebo already on.

Aiden.

I sit on a bench and watch everyone bustling around. People exit the grocery store, their bags overflowing. Mr. and Mrs. Harper,

Jack's parents, walk out carrying a jug of eggnog. The bell above Cup o' Jo's door jingles as people stroll out, holding warm beverages. At the bookstore, people stream in and out, clutching their purchases tightly. Everyone seems so happy.

The lights on the tree wink at me.

Aiden.

I take out my phone, turn it back on. Sam has sent half a dozen texts, but I ignore them, and scroll until I find the last message I sent to Aiden. Just an hour ago: *I'm here.*

And I was. I want to always be here for him. But I don't know if he wants me close to him at all.

I turn my phone off again and walk into Cup o' Jo. Inside, the shop is full of customers, some sitting at the tables, laughing and chatting, mugs steaming next to them. Others are getting their orders to go, carrying out cups and paper bags of baked goods. None of them are Aiden.

I almost leave, but Jo calls, "Emma!" She's at the counter, taking orders. "Peppermint mocha?"

"No . . ."

Jo eyes me.

"No, thank you," I say. "I'll have my usual. Peppermint hot chocolate. It's regular, but that's what makes it so special." The realization dawns on me.

"Are we still talking about peppermint hot chocolate?" she asks as she makes my drink.

"I'm . . . not totally sure. Aiden didn't happen to stop by . . . did he?"

"Nope, haven't seen him since the other night." Jo slides the mug to me, examining my face. "It would be nice to see the two of you in here together, though. Like old times!" She pauses. "Well, except that you have a boyfriend now. Where is he, by the way?" She peers around me.

"He's not here," I say. Which isn't a lie. I don't have a boyfriend with me. I don't have a boyfriend at all.

The customer behind me huffs impatiently, so I pay for my drink and tell Jo a quick thanks, then move out of the way. But I can still feel Jo's eyes on me.

There is a little space open on the couch by the fire, so I sit down and drink my hot chocolate, the mint tingling my lips, and reminding me of all the ghosts. I finish the drink quickly, feeling too haunted to stay for long. Jo is busy behind the counter and doesn't see me leave.

I walk through Briar Glen slowly, past houses whose familiarity should bring me comfort, but I just feel homesick. How can I feel homesick for a place I'm already in?

I round the corner to my street, and something is sitting on my porch. As I get closer, I realize it's not a something, but a some*one*.

Sam.

He stands up when I'm a few feet away from the porch. His snowboard and duffel bag are behind him. He's bundled up in his coat, hat, and gloves. It strikes me how we were both in T-shirts and shorts when we first met. How different things were then.

The anger that contorted his face earlier is gone, replaced by another expression I don't recognize: sadness.

"Emma." He's hoarse, his voice barely a whisper. "I'm so sorry."

I'm still angry—angrier than I've ever been in my life—but one of my hard edges starts to soften. "What are you even apologizing for?" I ask, not angrily, but with resignation.

"Take your pick. A: for pushing Aiden; B: for lying about pushing Aiden; C: for all the terrible things I said to Aiden and to you; or D: all of the above."

"I'm going to go with D."

"Yeah, that's what I thought." His voice is still so quiet.

I cross my arms, and he says, "I was jealous. It's no excuse, but the way you and Aiden look at each other—"

I frown. "Look at each other? We've been friends for forever. I look at him all the time. Or I did . . ."

Sam shakes his head. "It's not just the history with you guys. It's not just the past. It's the present. And the future."

My heart thuds in my chest. "I still don't know what you're talking about."

"You're never going to love me the way you love Aiden." He sighs. "And . . . and that's okay."

My mouth drops open. "Love?" I sputter. "But we're . . . but you and me . . ." The words in my head are doing a confusing dance with the feeling in my chest.

A car honks, and I turn around.

"Where . . . where are you going?" I ask.

"I called a ride to the train station." Sam picks up his bag and snowboard. "Listen . . . maybe when Aiden comes to visit you, I can show him around? Try to make it up to him?"

"Aiden visiting? He hates the city." I say it automatically. Sam walks down the steps, and my brain plays catch up. "Wait, you're leaving?"

Sam chuckles softly. "Yeah."

"Because we broke up." My brain starts to move a little more quickly. "Oh, Sam, we broke up." The words hurt, and I'm crying, but the pain doesn't feel like it's going to knock me over the way it did when I thought about how much I missed Aiden.

Sam is right in front of me now. He puts down his stuff, peers at me with those puppy-dog eyes. Whatever it was I used to feel when he looked at me seems to have evaporated. I think it happened when I heard him talking to Aiden at the rink.

We stare at each other, and the car honks again. "Are we cool?" he asks.

"I'm not sure," I say honestly. "But I think we will be eventually."

"Good." He nods and smiles. "I'll see you back at Easton."

"Right," is all I can say.

I watch him get in the car. As soon as it pulls away, my front door flies open.

"Finally!" Kerry stands there, looking bewildered. "Can you please tell me what is going on?"

I cautiously step inside. The house is eerily quiet. "Where are Mom and Dad?"

"Christmas shopping. They left when you were ice-skating," she says impatiently.

Ice-skating. It already feels like it was a million years ago.

"Which your boyfriend came back from alone. He told me he wouldn't be able to go to the winter festival after all, that he needed to see his family today. He packed his stuff, then he called a car, and then you showed up." She huffs. "So let me repeat my question: What is going on?"

"That's just it," I say. "I don't have a boyfriend anymore."

"What?" Kerry waits for me to elaborate. "Does any of this have anything to do with me telling you to follow your heart?" she asks. "Not that I want to take credit for any decisions you made, but maybe I also kind of want to, especially if they're good decisions."

I laugh a shallow laugh.

"Okay, I'm done joking. Are you okay?" Kerry asks, using a more serious tone this time.

I say tentatively, "I don't know."

"Right," Kerry says with a nod. "Then we better get the cookies."

A few minutes later, we're sitting on the couch, eating messily decorated sugar cookies, *How the Grinch Stole Christmas* on in the background. I tell her about the party, about what happened at the rink.

The movie is at the part where the Grinch feels his heart growing, and I'm just telling Kerry that Sam told Aiden he wasn't good enough for me, when I hear a light scratching at the back door.

I figure it's the wind, pushing a tree branch against the door, but the scratching continues. I pause the movie, the image of the Grinch's growing heart frozen on the TV screen.

I open the door, and I can't believe who is standing there.

12
AIDEN

I yank off my skates and return them in a fog, then leave the rink, not even sure where I'm going. But at least I'm going somewhere, and not just standing still.

I walk home the long way. I deliberately avoid the town square and Cup o' Jo. I can't think of a time I've ever needed a peppermint hot chocolate more, or a time that drinking one would make me feel worse.

When I get home, Mackerel is in the front window, and when I walk inside, he meets me in the mudroom, wagging his tail and jumping up to lick my face.

"What's all the commotion?" Grandma asks, poking her head around the corner of the room.

Mackerel runs over to her, panting happily, and it's like he's excited to tell her that I'm home. "Oh, to be a dog," she says.

"Tell me about it."

"I'd much rather you tell me what's going on with you." She walks out of the room before I can protest or ask her how she knows anything is going on with me, and I find myself joining her in the living room, where she's wrapping presents. Mack follows, too, and curls up by my feet.

"Where is everyone?" I ask.

"What, I'm not good enough for you?"

I can't help but chuckle. "Of course you are, Grandma."

She nods. "Your grandpa and dad are working at the holiday market, and your mom is meeting one of her people for coffee."

"Her people?"

"The people she works with," she says impatiently, waving her hand.

"Clients?" I supply.

"That's it!" She neatly cuts a piece of paper and begins to wrap it around a box and says without looking up, "I know I always say people should mind their own business, and I don't want to be one of those nosy grandparents, but I can tell something is bothering you, and believe me, the more you keep that stuff bottled up, the worse it'll get."

She stops wrapping the present and puts her hands together, then pulls them apart, miming an explosion.

"Boom," she says. "Stress will kill you, you know."

"Thanks, Grandma . . . I think?"

She goes back to wrapping. I'm still trying to figure out how to put into words what just happened with Emma when she says, "So talking about something when it's bothering you usually helps, but I'm also not going to force you to tell me anything."

"It's Emma."

"That's what I thought. That boyfriend of hers is no good."

"Why do you say that?"

She shrugs. "I've seen his type all my life. Arrogant."

"Did you talk to him?" I ask in surprise.

"Didn't need to. I heard him talking at the party and that was enough for me." She cuts another piece of paper decisively and picks up the tape.

I didn't even see my grandparents at the holiday party, so I'm not sure when Grandma heard Sam, and then I remember I left before she did.

"I don't know what Emma sees in him," she goes on.

"He seems to make her happy."

You're not good enough for her.

"Happy?" She snorts. "That girl was miserable at the party."

"She was probably just tired." Why am I defending her relationship?

You're not good enough for her.

Grandma puts down her tape and looks at me. "Aiden, you're not fooling anyone. You hate the guy."

"I don't!" I say quickly, unsure if what I'm saying is true. "I want to support her."

"Sure you do."

"Even Mack isn't too crazy about him!"

Mack wags his tail when he hears his name.

"You heard your grandpa: Never trust a man who says he's not an animal guy."

"I thought he was kidding?"

"Behind every joke there's a truth." She picks up the scissors. "And I know it's not just a jealousy thing, either," she says after a moment.

"Jealousy?" I echo.

"Yeah," she says. "Why you don't like the guy. Okay, maybe you're a little jealous, but I think you can tell he's no good for Emma."

"He's no good in general!" I say with sudden anger. "He knocked me over at the ice-skating rink, denied it, and told *me* I'm not good enough for Emma. She even heard him say the last part, too!" My words practically spill out of me.

Grandma's face turns a shade of crimson. "Little creep," she mutters. "But let me guess, Emma didn't see the push?"

"Were you at the skating rink, too?" I sputter.

She chuckles. "I know I may seem old, but I was young, too, once."

I groan. "Please don't tell me about you being a teenager in love, too."

"What? Why would I tell you that? That's personal!"

"Never mind." I don't want to think any more about my conversation with Dad. "But that's exactly what happened," I continue.

"Like I said, I've seen his type a million times," Grandma says, resuming her gift wrapping. "You can't let him get under your skin."

"Even when he pushes me and lies about it?" I feel my anger returning.

She takes a deep breath. "Listen, I would love to give him a piece of my mind myself and tell him if he ever touches you again, I'll—"

"Grandma!" I interject.

"You have to be the bigger person. Emma's a smart girl. She'll figure out he's no good."

"She hasn't yet, though. They've been dating since the summer," I point out.

She studies my face. "I have a feeling coming back to Briar Glen might have helped her realize he's not the guy for her."

"Why do you say that?"

"Because I was—"

"Young once, too," I say in a hurry. "I know, I know."

"And it's clear you're head over heels for each other."

"Did you say . . . *each other*?"

Grandma laughs again. "I did. But you can't force anyone to admit their feelings."

"Really? I kind of feel like that's what you're doing with me," I joke.

"Nah, I don't need you to admit anything. It's written all over your face. And it's been written all over your face for years."

"Years?" I say weakly.

"Yep," she says, concentrating on her wrapping again.

"So . . . what do I do?"

"About what?"

"My feelings. The last I saw Emma, I told her to leave me alone."

"Then take the space you need," she says simply. "Those feelings aren't going anywhere."

"So I just sit around and wait?"

"I didn't say anything about waiting!" she says. "No, the best thing to do when you're trying not to think about love is to do something else. Why don't you work on your music?"

I sigh. "But every time I play guitar I think of Emma."

"Then find another thing!" she says with a wave of her hand. "Do something you've never done before with Emma. No associations!"

"No associations," I repeat.

"Didn't you say you're in the sled race?"

"Yeah . . ." With everything that had happened with Emma I'd almost forgotten. "But that's something Emma and I used to do together. And remember when I fell off the sled? Emma was the first one up the hill to make sure I was okay. There's definitely an association there." I feel my face reddening as I remember the embarrassment that followed me for weeks.

"Yes, but have you ever entered the sled race since then?" she asks wisely.

"No," I say slowly.

"So there you go. Think about that."

"But how?"

"Have you ever entered the sled race since you fell off your sled?"

"You just asked me, Grandma," I say, studying her face carefully. "Are you feeling okay?"

"Yes, of course," she confirms. "I'm not batty! But seeing as how you haven't raced in two years, and last time you did you fell off your sled, it seems like something you might want to, I don't know, practice?"

I think about standing at the top of the hill, holding my sled, and then flash back to two years ago, my sprained wrist, the horror of the entire town seeing my fall. My hands start to sweat. "Maybe I shouldn't race?"

"That's nonsense. Don't let fear win. You can't spend the rest of your life avoiding getting on a sled, you know. Especially considering the family business." She snorts. "As much as I enjoy the irony of a grandson who sells sleds but is afraid of them!"

"I know, I know," I say impatiently, hating that she's right. But something else is bugging me.

"Something else you're afraid of?" Grandma asks.

"How do you do that?"

"I don't read your mind; I read your face. Spit it out."

I sigh heavily. "I think part of the reason Emma liked Sam is because he's so different. He's from the city, and he loves school like Emma, and he's been taking her to all these supposedly incredible places to eat—"

"Ah, she got swept up with a city boy."

"Yeah, I guess."

"You know that doesn't make him better than you, right?" She's stopped wrapping presents and looks at me earnestly.

I nod.

"Because you'd do fine in the city. If that's where you want to go. But I don't think it is."

"No, I can't leave Briar Glen."

Grandma looks at me skeptically. "Can't? Or don't want to?"

"I mean, both!" I'm frustrated that I have to explain something so obvious to her. "The family business is here. All of our family is here. I'm not leaving that."

"Oh, Aiden." She puts her hands on my face. "Your heart is bigger than your brain sometimes. Of course you can leave. Don't think about stuff like family business yet. You have your whole life ahead of you."

"But doesn't everyone need me here?" I hear the smallness in my voice.

Grandma pats my cheek. "The only thing we need is for you to be happy. Wherever that is!"

"Really?"

"Yes!" She knocks lightly on my head. "Try thinking with this thing a little more than that thing in your chest, okay?"

"Okay, Grandma."

"Good boy." She pats my cheek one more time, then continues wrapping presents.

Mackerel is asleep, chasing something in his dream. I stand up and wipe my sweaty hands on my pants, and he rouses.

"I should practice," I say, more to myself than to Grandma.

"What am I always telling you?"

"There is nothing to fear but fear itself," I recite, looking at Mackerel. He wags his tail and takes the spot where I was just sitting on the couch. "Seat stealer."

He thumps his tail in response.

"If anyone asks, I'll tell them where you are," Grandma says.

"Who would ask?"

"You never know!" she says mysteriously.

I pull on my warmest coat, snow pants, hat, and, at the last minute, my Emma gloves. I head out to the garage and open it to find a row of shiny sleds. I breathe deeply and grab the nearest one.

ELEVEN MONTHS AGO.

The last bell rang, and Aiden practically shot out of his chemistry lab chair. It was the end of the first week back to school after the holiday break, and Aiden felt like it'd been a year already.

He bumped into Scarlet, apologizing to her as he hurried out of the room.

Just before he left the classroom, though, he saw Emma talking to their chemistry teacher, Mr. Moore, and realized he was hurrying for nothing.

He waited in the hallway, boring eye laser beams through Emma, but she just kept talking. Aiden eventually gave up and went to his locker, which was down the hall from the chemistry lab.

After Aiden had rearranged and reorganized his locker for the third time, Emma walked out of the classroom, telling Mr. Moore to have a good weekend.

She saw Aiden at his locker and said, "Thanks for waiting. I was just talking to Mr. Moore about money. Did you know that it doesn't really smell?"

"Huh?" Aiden asked.

"Well, coin money, anyway. Metallic money."

Aiden wrinkled his nose. "Yeah, it does. It stinks. Or are you going to tell me that there is something that only humans can smell, like how only dogs can hear a dog whistle?"

Emma blinked at Aiden, one side of her mouth turning up in a smile. "No, but that is a really cool guess."

"I thought I'd try."

"But you're not totally far off. When you smell coins, you're smelling the compounds that are formed from things like sweat. The metal just causes the reaction. Isn't that cool?"

Emma could make anything sound cool or interesting. "Sure," Aiden said easily. "Also slightly disgusting."

"We mammals lead disgusting lives. Though, insects and fungi are pretty gross, too. Have I told you about *Ophiocordyceps unilateralis*? The zombie-ant fungus?"

"No, and please don't."

Emma laughed. "Okay, okay. I just need to stop by my locker and I'll be ready."

"No rush," Aiden said. And he meant it. He'd take any time

with Emma he could get, even if it was just keeping her company while she packed her backpack.

They walked to her locker, Emma still talking about the smelly coin thing, and she distractedly took books out of her locker and put them into her bag. Then she looked down, realized she had too many, and put some of the books back in her locker. Finally, she said, "Ready!"

"That was the longest week ever! I can't believe it's only January 7. It feels like January 49."

Emma lightly whacked Aiden with her glove before she put it on. "I think I know what you need."

"I do, too—to get out of here."

"You know what I meant," Emma said, referencing their Cup o' Jo Friday tradition.

They exited the school, walking slowly on the sidewalk, just in case they found any icy patches, and stepping carefully over the snowbanks. Aiden's hands felt warm in the gloves Emma had given him for Christmas. He told Emma about the song he was learning on guitar, another Green Day song, and Emma said she couldn't wait to hear him play it.

By the time they got to Cup o' Jo a few minutes later, they were more than ready for warm drinks. Lucy looked up from behind the counter as the door jingled open and Emma and Aiden walked in.

“Hmm, let me guess,” Lucy said, putting her hand on her chin, pretending to think. “Two pumpkin spice lattes?”

“Maybe next time,” Aiden and Emma said in unison.

Lucy arched an eyebrow at them, and Aiden felt himself blushing. Emma busied herself rummaging through her backpack. When she looked up, her face was flushed. She held a wad of cash. “My treat, this time.”

Aiden grabbed their drinks, and they walked past other tables, where some people were tapping away at laptops, and where families with little kids sat, drinking hot chocolate.

Miraculously, the couch by the fireplace was open, so they sat there. Emma and Aiden set their mugs down on the table, then took off their coats. There was a lock of hair that had slipped out of Emma’s short ponytail, and Aiden lifted his hand to push it off her face, but quickly let his hand drop to his lap. He still had his gloves on. And it would have been weird to touch Emma’s face.

Emma chuckled. “I guess you like the gloves?”

“They’re great,” he said, still feeling uncomfortable.

Emma watched Aiden remove his gloves carefully, almost tenderly. She looked at his hands, which she’d seen a million times, but for some reason they seemed different now. Softer. She wondered if she could touch him, to see if his skin was as soft as it looked, but she shoved the thought out of her mind.

"What are you up to this weekend?" Emma asked, trying to stop thinking about Aiden's soft skin.

Aiden was confused. They didn't usually talk about weekend plans; they just *had* weekend plans together. "Probably the same thing I do every weekend?" He gave Emma a funny look. "Helping my family at the market, taking Mack for a walk, trying to learn a darn Green Day song, hanging out with you?"

Emma nodded, trying to focus on his words.

"And what are *you* up to this weekend?"

It felt so odd to talk to Emma this way, like they weren't acutely aware of everything happening in the other's life. Even the thought of it made Aiden wrap his hands more tightly around his mug of peppermint hot chocolate.

"Well . . . that application is due on Monday, so I'll probably finish it up." Emma's words came out in a rush. "I mean I've reread my essay, like, fifty times, but I think I'll actually hit the submit button this weekend."

Aiden racked his brain. "And this is the application for . . ."

"Aiden! Please tell me you're kidding!" Emma's feet bounced up and down next to Aiden's, and one of those bouncing feet hit Aiden's shin. They wore thick winter boots, but they felt the contact, and pulled their feet away from each other.

It was just bright enough in Cup o' Jo that Emma could see the golden flecks in Aiden's eyes.

"Emma?" Aiden said. She was gazing at him with such intensity that he couldn't tear his eyes away.

"Yes!" Emma said, breaking the eye contact as she put a spoon in her mug and started stirring. "That Easton Academy application."

Aiden felt some of the color drain from his face. Now he remembered. It was the application she had mentioned in the fall. He remembered the nagging feeling, and that other unnameable feeling. She hadn't brought the school up since, though, so he thought she had changed her mind, or forgotten about it.

"Right!" Aiden said. "You're still thinking of applying?" He hoped he sounded supportive. Because he was—of *course* he was—but the thought of Emma being at a different school, in a different state . . .

Emma frowned for just a second, then said cheerily, "Yep!" She worried that Aiden could hear the uncertainty in her voice.

Aiden thought back to just a few minutes ago in their conversation, when he'd had that odd sense of Emma being someone who didn't know everything he said or did. Everything he thought. The minutiae of his life. And if she moved away to New York, would that be the kind of friend she would become?

Someone who didn't have context for everything in Aiden's life? He shuddered a bit.

"Do you think it's a good idea for me to apply?" Emma asked.

Aiden wanted to say that she shouldn't apply, that he wanted to keep Emma just as close to him as she was now, but he knew that she wasn't anyone's to own. "Yes." He was surprised by her uncertainty.

"Really?" Emma's face was unreadable, like she'd been expecting a different reaction.

"It'll help you get ready for college, and it'll look really good on college applications."

"You sound like me!" said Emma.

Aiden felt that blush again. "Also, you're Emma Sherman. You can do anything you put your mind to. It's one of the reasons"—he caught himself—"why you're a good friend. You make me want to try harder at things. To be better."

"I do?" Emma bit her lip to hide the grin she could feel forming.

"Your determination is inspiring," Aiden said, his voice suddenly quiet.

Emma looked up, and Aiden once again felt the intensity of her gaze. "Thank you."

For as long as Aiden had known Emma, she had never looked at him like this before, and he felt goose bumps on his arms. Emma felt a warmth spreading throughout her.

This time Aiden broke the eye contact. "I've always wanted to visit New York City!" He tried to sound chipper. "This will give me a great reason to finally make the trip."

"You have?"

"Okay, not really. But *now* I want to visit!" As he said the words, he felt like someone else was speaking. "Even if it's crowded, loud, and smelly."

"It's only smelly in the summer!"

"Oh good, so you wouldn't have to worry about that," Aiden said.

"I wouldn't?"

Aiden chuckled uncomfortably. "You'd be going to the school in the fall. Hopefully past the worst of the stinky season."

Emma didn't say anything, though.

"What?" Aiden finally asked.

"They also have a summer program, so I could start right after school ends."

"Oh!" Aiden said so loudly that one of the people on their laptops turned to look at them.

"But I probably wouldn't do that. And I probably won't get in, anyway!"

They were both quiet again.

Aiden struggled for something to say, then wondered why Emma wasn't saying more. "Can I ask you a question?" Aiden said carefully.

Emma said with a faint smile on her face, "You just did?"

"Seriously, though, why are you applying?"

Emma seemed to come back to life now. "It's like I said before—like *you* said before. It would open so many doors for me. Their academics are intense, and I'd learn so much, and it'd help me get into a good college, maybe even an Ivy. Plus, it's New York!" Emma didn't think this last part required any further explanation, but she kept going, "I could see plays on Broadway; Off Broadway; Off-Off Broadway; I could go to the American Museum of Natural History or MoMA or the Whitney or any museum I want, whenever I want."

Emma's eyes gleamed, and Aiden couldn't resist a laugh. "And when will you go to classes and study?"

"I'd have tons of time for that, too! I'd be living on campus, so I'd be super close to the library and my classrooms. Can you imagine?" But as she said the last part, she felt some of her enthusiasm fading.

Living on campus. The words felt strange in her mouth, and even stranger as she said them. She had never lived anywhere but

Briar Glen, anywhere but the room she currently lived in. Still, though, she had Aiden's support, and she knew her best friend wouldn't encourage her to do something she didn't want to or couldn't do.

But as she looked at Aiden, she had a lightning-bolt thought: *What if Aiden wanted her to go? Maybe he wanted her to apply to Easton because he wanted space from her?* The thoughts felt even more ridiculous than the words she'd just said, and they were not the way her brain usually operated.

Aiden felt himself light up as he listened to Emma. Her joy had a way of spreading to him as well. But then reality came crashing back as she talked about her dorm room. *Would it ever be a room he'd see? Would she have a roommate? Who would this person be?* And boarding school meant . . . school. Meant he wouldn't be at Briar Glen High with Emma anymore. He'd never navigated school without her before, and to think about finishing high school without her . . . it created an odd feeling in his stomach.

And then, as he looked at Emma, her face lit up, her eyes sparkling, her Emma-ness, he had a split-second thought: *Was she so excited about Easton because she wanted to get away from him?* It felt absurd, but it also felt absurd to think about Briar Glen without Emma.

“You okay?” Emma asked Aiden. She was in the middle of telling him about the small class sizes at Easton but stopped mid-sentence.

Aiden forced a happy face. “Yep! It’s just a lot of information at once. I don’t mean that in a bad way. I’m just trying to process.”

Emma studied Aiden. Could she really move to New York City without him? There was some part of her that wished Aiden wanted to go to Easton, too, that they could apply together, but that would be un-Aiden-ish. He tolerated school, but he didn’t love it the way Emma did. He didn’t get excited to study for tests, to write papers. He wasn’t always asking for extra work from their teachers like Emma was.

Emma forced herself to concentrate. “The admissions are super selective! There is a really good chance I won’t even get in. I think maybe part of why I’m applying is to prove that I can? To my parents, to my sister. She’s so perfect, wanting to become a lawyer, and maybe I just want to remind everyone that I’m smart, too?” She felt slightly ashamed about what she’d just admitted, but Aiden didn’t seem fazed.

“And you want to uproot and change everything about your life because you’re trying to prove something?” he asked.

“No! Of course not. I don’t think so. Anyway, like I said, I probably won’t get in, so we don’t need to talk about this anymore!" She took another sip of her hot chocolate. "Now can I please tell you about the zombie-ant fungus? Pretty please?"

Aiden snickered. "Okay, okay."

But that way she had looked at him, Aiden knew he'd do anything she asked him, whatever she needed, and the realization scared him a bit.

13

EMMA

"Mackerel!" I say, opening the back door. "What are you doing here?"

In response, he's on his hind legs, licking my face, and I brace myself against the counter so I don't fall over.

"Mack!" I say, giggling. "I've missed you, too."

He sits down, tail wagging, looking at me, his left ear sticking up.

"Mack!" Kerry says, walking into the kitchen. "Well, if that isn't a sign."

He bounds over to her now, wiggling and licking her face. She sits on the ground and he circles around her, bumping her with his nose.

"A sign of what?" I ask Kerry.

"Duh." Kerry holds Mack's head away from her face so she can talk between his licks. "A sign that maybe you should be with Aiden?"

"Like hang out with him?"

"Emma, for someone so smart you can be a little obtuse sometimes. You were just telling me what Sam said to Aiden, what he did. Nothing justifies any of it, but can I guess the reason you don't have a boyfriend anymore?"

Mack sits down, satisfied that he's thoroughly cleaned Kerry's face.

"Yeah, because of what he did to Aiden!"

I remember the hurt on his face.

Leave me alone.

I remember the conversation I just had with Sam. *I was jealous.*

"And why do you think he would do something so horrible? What is Mom always telling us?"

"Jealous," I say in a daze. "He was jealous. He told me. And Mom always says when someone is being cruel, it's about them and not a reflection of you."

You're never going to love me the way you love Aiden.

But I didn't need Sam to point it out to me. I knew it all along.

"Exactly!" Kerry says. "Whenever Kristy and I get snippy with each other, it's usually because one of us is having a bad day, or something happened that upset one of us—"

"I need to be with Aiden." The words pop out of my mouth.

"Normally I'd call you out for interrupting me when I'm telling you something so personal but—"

"I need to be with Aiden." The words gather strength.

"And again I'll pardon the interruption."

I'm out of the room before she can say anything else, grabbing my coat off the rack and sliding my boots on. I'm about to head out the front door when Mack comes trotting in.

"I think you forgot something," Kerry says, following Mack. "Your sign?"

Mack sits down again and looks at us, panting.

"Do you ever feel like Mackerel understands what we're saying?" Kerry asks.

"I don't just feel like it. I know it." Mack hops up again, and I say, "Okay, I'll take you home. To Aiden."

"Good luck."

"Luck? Seriously?" I say with alarm.

"No, not luck. You don't need it. Can I say one thing again?"

"What?" My patience is starting to shred.

"Follow your heart."

"What do you think I'm doing?" But then I run over to Kerry and give her a big hug. It's a bit awkward at first, but she wraps her arms around me. "Thank you."

"Just get over to Aiden's house!" Kerry says, releasing me.

I laugh and pat my leg, and Mack follows me out the front door.

We walk quickly, him next to me, looking up at me every few paces. "I can't believe Aiden trained you to walk without a leash."

Mack wags his tail and sneezes into the snow.

"Actually, yeah, I can. Aiden really can do anything. I don't think he realizes how much he can do. The way he helps his grandpa and dad at the market, how important his family is to him, how important he is to his family. How fast he picks up songs on the guitar. What a good . . . friend he is." I hear my voice catch on the last words. "He's never judged me, or not been there for me. He listens, he makes me laugh. My god I've missed him."

I don't realize I'm crying until I feel the tears falling off my cheeks.

"Oh, Mack," I say, bending down and sticking my face in his fur. I put my arms around him, and we just stay like that for a moment, until he stands, ending the hug.

"You're right, let's keep going. I need to be with Aiden."

I pick up my pace, and Mack trots along. "If he'll let me," I whisper.

In a few minutes we're at Aiden's house. My nerves jangle, and my hands sweat inside my gloves.

Mack runs up the porch steps ahead of me, and I take a deep breath. I ring the doorbell.

"Hold on!" Aiden's grandma calls, and then I hear her brisk footsteps.

When she opens the door, she seems just as startled to see me as she does Mack.

"When did you sneak out?" she asks Mackerel, but he just wags his tail. "Must have been when Aiden left," she mutters.

"Aiden left?"

She squints up at me. "He didn't go far. Just to the park."

"Oh, okay," I say.

"He did take a sled with him, though."

"He did? Why?"

"Why do you think? To go sledding!"

"But what about his sledding accident? He's been afraid of sledding ever since!"

She shrugs. "He said he was ready to face the hill. Like I've been telling him, the only thing he should be afraid of is fear. And I don't think it was the hill he was afraid of, anyway."

"Is he going to be okay?" I ask, feeling a rising sense of panic.

"Of course he will! He's Aiden."

"No, I know that. I just mean . . ." I don't know what I mean.

"You can grab a sled from the garage if you want. Take Mack

with you, too, will you? I'm not surprised he showed up at your door. He's been pacing around the house since Aiden left. I think he's nervous, too."

"Why would he be nervous?" I hear the nervousness in my own voice.

"Aiden? Or Mackerel?"

"Either. Both. I don't know! I think I have to go to the park."

"I think you should go to the park."

"Okay. I'm going to the park."

"Don't forget a sled. I'll open the garage for you!" she calls as I run down the porch steps, Mackerel behind me.

The garage door slowly creaks open, and there are about a half-dozen sleds. I grab one, and I start running. Well, as fast as I can, dragging a sled behind me, Mackerel right next to me.

The park is only about five minutes away, but it's the longest five minutes of my life. I think about Aiden's wrist injury two years ago. It was a minor injury, but if he somehow gets hurt worse I'll never forgive myself. It's bad enough what Sam did to him.

I have to save him.

It's a wild thought. But, finally, we get to the park. And I see Aiden.

14

AIDEN

I expect the park to be crowded, but there are just a few groups of people sledding down the hill. The registration booth for tomorrow is already set up, and the banner hanging reads:

BRIAR GLEN'S 44TH ANNUAL WINTER FESTIVAL!

I look at the hill, inhale deeply, and start walking slowly, pulling my sled behind me.

I stop, turn around, and my hands start sweating in my gloves. I remember Jason, Graham, and Dustin, how ruthlessly they teased me for falling off my sled, for weeks. Emma sticking up for me, which just made them tease me even more. They eventually got sent to the principal's office, and then they finally stopped.

I feel dizzy for a second, but I turn around again and keep going up. I slip once, but catch myself, and still I keep going. There is a group of kids about twenty feet away from me sledding, laughing, and cheering, but I can't look at them and lose my concentration. I reach the top, but I'm not ready to look down, to remember the last time I was here, the embarrassment, the shame. My hands feel even sweatier in my gloves, and I hold the rope of my sled tighter. Slowly, taking baby steps, I turn around, and I feel dizzy again. I put my sled on the ground, but I remain standing, not ready to set my body on the sled just yet.

The view is quite nice. I can almost see to the town square. I picture it, people walking around, *ooh*ing and *aah*ing at the tree, at the lights my family put up. It would make more sense for me to be there. What am I doing, really? Maybe Grandma *is* batty, telling me to come here.

I'm starting to rethink my plan, then realize I didn't even really make a plan to begin with. Sled down the hill. Then what? How many times will it take before I can shake off the dread mixed with embarrassment every time I think about what happened two years ago? How many times will it take before I stop thinking about Emma?

The last of the sledders are done, piling into a minivan. I'm envious of them. I wonder if they're going to Cup o' Jo for hot chocolate or some kind of other warm treat. I'd really, really rather be at Cup o' Jo than at the top of this hill. But Cup o' Jo makes me think of Emma, and thinking of Emma reminds me of Sam knocking me over.

You're not good enough for her.

I may not know why I'm at the top of this hill or what I'm going to do next, but at least it gives me something else to think about, to do.

I look down again, at the bottom of the hill, and I see a black dog that looks kind of like Mackerel standing with someone. The person's coat looks like a coat I've seen before, I think. Then I hear the dog barking, and it sounds like Mackerel, and then I realize—it *is* Mackerel.

What is he doing here? And who is he with?

"Aiden!" the person shouts.

Not just any person. It's Emma.

"Why are you here?" The wind carries my words away.

She shouts something back, but I can't hear her, either.

She starts climbing up the hill, Mackerel following behind her.

I watch her, not sure what she's doing, not sure what I should say.

She keeps climbing. She and Mack are getting closer, Mack's snout covered in snow. Emma shouts, "Let me help you! I don't want you to get hurt!"

I stand there, completely baffled at why she's here. Mack reaches me, wiggling, and he's up on his hind legs, almost knocking me over. "Mackerel? Do you know what's going on?"

"Aiden," Emma shouts again, even closer now, "wait!"

I remember, though: I'm here to forget about Emma. I can't keep waiting for her. So I sit on the sled.

I hear Emma shouting, "No, don't go!"

But it's too late.

I grab the rope and start flying down the hill.

I hear something behind me, but I won't turn around. I won't fall off a sled again. Snow is spraying everywhere, and I can't believe how fast I'm going . . . and I forgot it's actually kind of . . . fun? I'm laughing.

It's the sound of a sled behind me. That's what I hear. And it's catching up. Emma shouts, "Slow down!" And it's her. She's right behind me.

Suddenly, I remember I haven't been on a sled in two years, and last time I was on one I got hurt.

I give a quick glance behind me.

"Turn around!" Emma shouts in a panic. "Look where you're going!"

It's too late. I turn just in time to see the snowbank, before I crash into it.

"Aiden!" she shouts for the millionth time as she comes to a stop at the bottom of the hill. She hops off her sled and runs over to where I am, in the snowbank. The snow is so deep that I can't move.

I hear something behind me in the snow, and it's Mackerel, using his body as a sled to come whooshing down the hill. He's on his side, face in the snow, flakes flying out around his body. It's such a ridiculous sight that I laugh. He stops at the bottom of the hill, shakes himself off, and hops through the snow to me. He's next to me within seconds, licking my face.

"Are you okay?" Emma asks, kneeling at my side.

"What are you doing here?" I ask. Mackerel stops attacking my face with his tongue and sits in my lap.

"I was worried!"

"About what?"

"It doesn't matter. Are you hurt? That's the most important thing to figure out now."

"Hurt? No? Why would I be? Also, me getting knocked over by your boyfriend wasn't enough for you today? You wanted to make sure I hit a snowbank, too? But right, the first thing didn't actually happen, according to your boyfriend." My earlier humor is gone.

"*Ex*-boyfriend," she says. "I'm so sorry. I know what happened. I heard what Sam said to you, too, but you told me to leave you alone, and he isn't right for me. And he won't be in the race tomorrow, either. He's on his way to meet his parents now. Early." She's trying to get the words out quickly.

"What?"

"It's all irrelevant! Can you tell me what your name is? What day of the week it is? Does anything hurt?"

"Emma," I say.

"That's my name!" she says in alarm.

"Emma!" I say again, laughing.

"Oh, you know your name! Wait, you're saying my name?"

"Yes I am, Emma."

We're so close to each other that I can feel her breath on my cheek, and I wonder if she can feel mine.

"It's Tuesday," I say in a soft voice.

"No!" Emma says, her laughter gone. "It's Wednesday."

"No, it's Tuesday."

Emma thinks for a second, and she realizes I'm right. "Wait, are you messing with me?"

I laugh again, harder, but Emma isn't laughing.

"Are you sure your head is okay?" she asks tentatively. "Because there is this thing, I forget the name of it, but it's a neurological issue caused by a head injury that presents itself as uncontrollable laughter."

I stop laughing. "Nah, I can control my laughter, see?"

"You're really okay? You hit that snowbank hard."

"Yep." I move my arms, my legs, brush snow off myself. Mackerel stands up and starts licking my face again. "Now can you please tell me why you're here and why my dog was with you?"

"He showed up at my door! I tried to bring him home, and your grandma said you were here with a sled, so Mackerel and I came here, and there you were, and I thought you were afraid of sledding?"

"And when you saw me at the top of the hill, your solution was to chase me on your own sled?"

"I guess so!" she says with exasperation. "I chased you on a sled." The realization becomes clear in her mind.

"You chased me on a sled," I repeat slowly. "We were in a sled *chase*."

"And Mackerel used his body as a sled," she says.

Mackerel looks up at us, proud of himself.

And we're laughing again.

"I've seen videos online of dogs doing it, but I never knew Mackerel was so skilled!" Emma says between fits of hysterics.

"If there is any dog who can sled down a hill, it's Mackerel." I pat his head.

Mackerel stands up and licks Emma's face and then mine, and then climbs back into my lap, even though he barely fits.

"But really, you still haven't told me why you're here."

"I told you, you haven't sledded in two years, and I was afraid you'd get hurt again, and I'm so sorry about Sam, and I'm sorry about everything, and I miss you, and I couldn't wait any longer to tell you. Which I guess is why I chased you down the hill on a sled."

"Well, that's one way to get your point across."

"That was pretty dramatic, wasn't it? But what if you'd gotten hurt again?"

"One, you know I didn't actually get that hurt two years ago, remember? I mean, it was mortifying. I know you know that part." I pause. "But my wrist was just sprained. Two, you know I crashed into the snowbank because I was looking back at you, right?"

"Oh," she says in a small voice. "Sorry?"

"I forgive you."

"And about Sam—"

"Maybe we don't have to talk about him anymore? I'm still recovering and all."

Emma snickers. "Why did you decide to enter the race, anyway?"

"I think I got tired of being afraid of things." I sigh. "And I think I needed to think about something that wasn't you."

"Why do you need to think about something that isn't me?" Her voice shakes.

"Because, Emma, I can't get you out of my mind." I gaze at her, the reality of my words sinking in with her.

"What do you mean?" she asks softly.

"I mean you're everywhere, Emma. Everything reminds me of you. School, my house, Cup o' Jo, every part of Briar Glen. You're here, but you're so far away." I play with the tag on Mackerel's collar. "I haven't been able to drink any peppermint hot chocolate since you moved to New York. I couldn't even go to Cup o' Jo when you first left."

Mackerel sits in my lap, watching the conversation.

Emma seems like she's about to say something, but I continue. "We all know that I'm not good enough for you. I suppose that's why you wanted to get away from me."

"What are you talking about?"

"What Sam said. I know I said I don't want to talk about him. But you heard him. I'm not good enough for you." I remember something else. "He also told me that it's a good thing you moved out of Briar Glen and met him." I hate the smallness of my voice.

"I sure picked a winner, didn't I?" she asks, putting her head in her palms. "But you know that's not true, don't you? Any of what he said?"

"It isn't?"

"No! But there's something he didn't mention."

"Oh? What's that?"

"Part of the reason I left . . . was because of you. Because of my *feelings* for you."

I'm not sure I've heard her right. "What feelings would those be?" I ask carefully.

"The feelings of . . ." she trails off again, looking away from me. "The feelings of I love my best friend, and I don't know what to do. I thought maybe if I moved away and started a new life for myself, maybe my feelings would go away. But they haven't. I wish it hadn't taken me dating Sam to figure out I couldn't keep it a secret any longer." She takes another deep breath but won't look at me.

Love.

I'm speechless. In the silence, Mackerel climbs out of my lap and looks at Emma, and then at me.

Emma goes on, quickly, "It's okay, you don't have to say anything. It's complicated and we're best friends and I hope I didn't just ruin everything."

"You didn't ruin anything," I say, finally finding my voice, my heart finally catching up.

Love.

"I started so many texts to you. Real ones. More than about what the city was like, about what I was learning at school. I wanted to tell you that I think I might apply to law school someday, too. But not because I'm competing with Kerry. I started looking into it, and there are so many different kinds of law, and I'd love to become an attorney who works for a nonprofit."

Her eyes gleam. I've forgotten how much she lights up when she talks about school, about her future. How could I have forgotten that?

"I'm getting off track," she says.

"Are you?" I say. "You know I always want to hear what you're planning for yourself, what you're thinking about."

"You do? Every time I brought up Easton you got quiet, so I figured you thought maybe I wouldn't get in or you were bored or—" There is so much earnestness in her eyes. "I don't know what I thought, actually."

"Of course not." I barely hear myself. "I knew you'd get in. I never doubted that. I was quiet because it was hard for me to think about you moving away. But I knew that was selfish, and I supported you, because I saw how happy you were when you got accepted, but then . . ."

"But then," Emma repeats.

Neither one of us needs to say anything else.

SIX MONTHS AGO.

The front door to Cup o' Jo was propped open, but it was warm inside. A fan rotated lazily on the ceiling. One lone customer sat at a table, a sweating lemonade next to their laptop.

Aiden waited at the counter, staring at the fireplace. Even though it wasn't lit, the fireplace made him feel even warmer.

Today was the day. He would tell her.

"Are you sure you and Emma want peppermint hot chocolates?" Jo asked Aiden skeptically.

He turned, distracted. "Yeah, that's fine."

"Aiden?" Jo asked.

"Hmm?" Aiden said, back to staring at the fireplace.

"You realize it's ninety degrees outside, right?"

He nodded. "If spicy food can cool off the body, maybe hot drinks can, too. Besides, it's a drink to celebrate the end of the school year, and I'd drink just about anything to celebrate that."

"Do you ever think someday you might miss high school?" Jo

looked wistful for a second. "I graduated over twenty years ago, and sometimes I wish I could do it again."

She had Aiden's attention now, and he was horrified. "Trust me," he said. "No you don't."

"You sound like Lucy." Jo laughed. "Emma is definitely coming?"

"Of course she is!" It came out more defensively than he intended, but she had to be coming today.

He had planned out what he was going to say to her. Had practiced on Mackerel and everything. He'd tell Emma how she filled his days with light and happiness, how he loved her curiosity, her ambition, her intelligence. He loved the way her eyes lit up and sparkled when she was excited about something. How kind she was, protective of him. The way she made him want to be a better person. And the way his body seemed to develop new nerve endings when they were together. How even just the lightest brush of her arm against his set off a firestorm inside his body. The way his ache for her was so strong it took his breath away.

He realized Jo was watching him and said, "Sorry, I know she's late a lot."

"It doesn't bother me. But it doesn't bug *you*?"

"I actually find it kind of interesting?"

"Interesting," she repeated thoughtfully.

"Yeah, it's not like she's late on purpose or doing it to be mean or anything. Sometimes she's talking to teachers; sometimes she's thinking about things. Whatever it is, she always has a good story."

"You are a very understanding friend."

"It's easy to be a good friend to her," Aiden said.

"Oh, yeah?" Jo had a wise look on her face that Aiden didn't fully trust.

"What?"

"I've known both of you guys a long time. I've known your friendship for a long time."

"We've been best friends. Since kindergarten."

"I know. Sometimes I can just sense things, is all. Working here, and as a parent. I knew Lucy and Jack liked each other the second I saw them talking."

"Even though she threw half a pie at his face?" Aiden asked, confused. "I don't want to throw a pie at Emma."

"Every love is a different love. And every love works in mysterious ways."

Aiden stared at Jo.

"I'm being so nosy! Forget I said anything!" Jo said abruptly. "Lucy told me I was turning into some kind of stereotypical nosy café owner, and I think she might be on to something."

Aiden laughed nervously. He was still thinking what to say next, thinking about what he was planning on telling Emma today, when she came rushing in, her face red. She wiped her sweaty hair off her forehead and clutched her phone with her other hand.

Aiden felt himself light up. Lately her presence had been doing that to him. Setting off something in his body that instantly made him happy and excited but comfortable and safe all at once.

"I . . . got . . . in!" Emma said between pants of air.

Aiden and Jo both gave Emma a bewildered look.

"To Easton!" Emma said, still panting.

The words weren't registering with Aiden. *Easton?* Then, his memory clicked into place.

"Oh!" he said. It came out as more of a squeak. Then, more loudly, "That's amazing, Emma!" Now his voice sounded too loud, but so did the words in his head.

New York City. Boarding school.

Emma didn't seem affected by the volume of his voice, though, or seem to have any idea what was going on in his head as she bounced up and down.

Jo frowned. "What is this?"

"It's this amazing, prestigious boarding school in New York City that I applied to, and I didn't think I'd get in because it's super competitive . . . but I did!" Emma said in a tumble of words.

Jo glanced at Aiden, but Aiden wasn't sure if he was quite comprehending Emma's words. There were too many of them all at once and none of them went with the words he'd planned on telling her today.

Emma looked at Aiden but quickly looked away again. If she saw even a flicker of doubt on his face, the whole thing would crumble, and she'd never be able to leave. And she needed to. Her heart was doing all kinds of funny things when she was with Aiden, and she didn't trust it. The words *the heart wants what it wants* were on a constant loop in her head, but she knew her heart might destroy her life if she followed it. Because following it would mean staying in Briar Glen and telling Aiden everything, and if he didn't feel the same way, it would ruin eleven years of friendship, and how many future years of friendship? No, the risk was too big. Going to Easton would put a stop to her feelings, and she'd be able to throw herself into her studies in a way she'd never done in Briar Glen.

Aiden heard himself saying, "Boarding school?" But the words didn't seem like they were coming from his mouth. They still didn't make any sense. Emma and Aiden were going to have peppermint hot chocolate now, just like they did almost every Friday, and they were going to talk about all the things they were going to do that summer: swim in the town pool, go for long walks in the woods with Mackerel, watch bad TV. Aiden would play guitar; Emma would practice the Ukrainian she was learning. But first he was going to tell her how he felt, and he'd finally get the words out of his heart, out of his brain.

As he saw how happy Emma was, how excited she was to be leaving, he realized his plan had been foolish. Foolish and dangerous. Because she must have realized how he was feeling, and that was why she was leaving. She couldn't wait to get away from him.

"I know, it's a shock!" Emma said. She studied Aiden's face, hoping to find some sort of excitement, some sort of happiness, but he just looked at her blankly.

Emma turned to Jo now, hoping for *someone* to be excited for her, but even Jo's face seemed strained.

Emma said, "Someone? Anything?"

Jo snapped out of it first. "That's incredible, Emma! We're going to miss you!"

Emma said, "Thank you!" but with far less enthusiasm than she'd had a few minutes ago.

Another customer walked in, so they paid for their drinks and then Emma grabbed them while Aiden just stood there. She sat at one of the tables, but Aiden remained motionless.

"Aiden? Want to sit here?"

He shook his head, snapping back to reality. “Sure.”

“I know it’s a lot to drop on you,” Emma said. “It’s a lot to drop on me! I just told my parents and Kerry and we’re trying to figure it all out, how and when I’ll get there.”

Aiden was still quiet.

“You could tell me congratulations?” Emma said, trying to joke, but Aiden’s face seemed to be made of stone.

“Congratulations,” Aiden said, without a hint of happiness to his voice.

Emma stared at her best friend in confusion. He’d told her he knew she’d get into Easton, but maybe he hadn’t been telling the truth? Was he really *that* surprised? He’d always been so encouraging. Had it all been a big lie?

Aiden knew he was being selfish, that this was an amazing opportunity for his friend, so he forced a smile and said, “Sorry! I’m happy for you. Of course I am! Congratulations!”

But Emma knew him too well. She knew he was lying.

They stared at each other, in an emotional standstill. A dark look crossed Emma’s face. His reaction just proved that what she was doing was right. Space from Aiden was what she needed. If she spent any more time with him, she might end up telling him how she felt. That she didn’t just want to spend time with him—she *needed* to spend time with him, the same way she needed air to breathe. That she loved the golden flecks in his hazel eyes, that she loved the way he listened to her, the way he kept her grounded with his practicality, how well they knew each other and what made the other person tick. How he learned Green Day songs because they were his parents' favorite band. The tender way he took care of Mackerel.

Aiden wanted to tell her he'd learned to play the song "Last Night on Earth" for her. That he thought about her when he played it. That everything in the song was about her. But he couldn't say any of that now.

"I've always said I can't just stay in Briar Glen forever!" Emma tried to make it sound like a joke.

"Yeah," Aiden said awkwardly. "I guess not."

Emma felt more of her enthusiasm fading. And doubt starting to sneak in. What had seemed, logically, like such a good plan was starting to make less and less sense. Could she really leave Briar Glen? Could she really leave *Aiden*? But, as she looked at him, could she really keep her feelings for him to herself anymore? Even more terrifying, though, was the thought of telling him. Or trying to tell him. How could she explain such a vast feeling as love?

"We just finished our sophomore year, and you're already planning your junior year! And beyond!" Aiden's voice sounded too loud to himself again.

"That's what happens in junior year. You start figuring out where you want to go to college. You start planning your life."

"What is there to plan?" Aiden asked. He wanted to tell her that he didn't understand her need to plan, because planning meant change, and she was already perfect the way she was.

Jo was at the far side of the counter, busying herself arranging the pastry case, trying not to listen to Aiden and Emma.

"I don't know, your future!" Emma could hear the doubt in her voice. She wanted to tell Aiden that she loved that he wasn't anxious about his future. How easily he went with the flow. That she loved his calmness. But she couldn't now.

"Emma, sometimes I think that you're so busy planning that you're not enjoying anything that's happening now."

Emma looked hurt and said, "Tell me, please, Aiden, what is there to enjoy right now? Let's see, I'm really loving the part where you're not excited for me about Easton."

"That's not what I meant."

"Well, why don't you tell me what you did mean? Or would that require too much planning for you?"

Emma's words felt like needles she was jabbing into Aiden's body, and he couldn't take it anymore. "Why are you turning this around on me? I'm not the one who is moving to New York City!"

"Yeah, something I thought you might be excited about for me, Aiden."

Aiden looked at her with such vulnerability, such openness, that she almost blurted out how she felt. But it was far too late to tell him any of that, though.

To Aiden's surprise he saw tears in Emma's eyes.

He couldn't believe he'd been about to tell her that he loved her.

"People need change!" Emma insisted. She heard the weakness in her words.

"No, Emma, I think you just *want* to change," Aiden said. "You've got to stop being afraid to live your life. The one you have now. Otherwise it's just going to pass you right on by."

"That is such a cliché, and you know it!"

For just the briefest of seconds, they both wondered if maybe there was hope that this conversation could end. They both almost smiled, but both seemed to remember what they were talking about at the same time.

"Listen, I thought you'd be happy for me, and you're not. But this isn't about me. It's about you. I can't let you hold me back anymore." As Emma said the words, she instantly knew she'd gone too far.

"Holding you back," Aiden said in a quiet voice. "That's what this friendship is to you? Me just holding you back?"

"No, Aiden, I'm sorry—"

But Aiden was already standing up. "I think I need to go."

"Wait!" Emma said, standing up, too.

But it was too late. Aiden was already walking out the door, and Emma just watched him leave. He left before she got a chance to tell him that the school also had a last-minute opening in the summer semester. Which was just a few days away. And which Emma now decided was an opening she was going to fill.

Neither one of them had touched their peppermint hot chocolates.

15

EMMA

"That was horrible," I say quietly.

"I hated it," Aiden said. "I thought *you* hated me."

The word stings. "How could I ever hate you?" I ask.

"I don't know. It didn't make sense. But nothing made sense."

We're both quiet again.

"I'm sorry—" we both start at the same time.

"You know you could have texted me to ask if I hated you," I say, but I'm smiling.

"Yeah, that would be a normal text for me to send." He smiles a small smile, too. "But I thought maybe you would know that I thought you hated me . . . somehow?"

"How would I know?" I say gently. "Then again, I thought you knew how I felt about you. But I guess not, but now I told you. Oh my god did I really just tell you I love you?" Reality smacks me in the face. "Wow, I just keep saying it, don't I? You know, maybe I should go." I stand.

Mackerel hops up on his hind legs, stretches his front paws on my knee.

"I love you, too," Aiden says.

I'm not sure I've heard him correctly. "What?"

Mackerel hops down and looks at me and starts wagging his tail.

"I wanted to tell you. I was going to tell you."

"When?" I say, throwing up my hands.

"The last time we went to Cup o' Jo together."

"When I told you about my acceptance to Easton," I say, stunned.

Aiden nods, and I sink back down to the ground, right next to him. Mack is still watching us, tail wagging.

"I didn't want to tell you how I felt and make things weird before you left, which is why I was so . . ."

"I thought you were mad at me for getting into Easton."

"Of course not!" he says. "I was so happy for you—*am* so happy for you—and all you're doing and learning. But I didn't see any point in telling you how I felt before you left. I didn't want you to think that I was trying to stop you from going. And the way you left, early, in *June*, without even saying—"

"I'm so sorry. I don't know what I was thinking. I wasn't thinking!"

"Before I even got that first text from you from the city, Jo was the one who told me that you left. She was at the market, getting a new cutting board," Aiden says.

"That's. . . ."

"Silly?" Aiden offers.

I cringe, thinking what the conversation must have been like. "Beyond ridiculous. I'm sorry."

Aiden says, "So both of us tried not to make things weird, and then you ended up starting at Easton early and leaving without either of us saying bye to each other. And then we barely talked for six months?"

"Well, when you put it like that . . ." I say. I realize how close we are, feel his warm breath on my cheek.

I lean toward him, and it's like every time I've dreamed about, except it's really happening. Our lips touch, lightly at first, and for a split second it feels so strange to be kissing Aiden, my best friend. But then I realize what feels so strange is that my dream is finally coming true. I'm kissing Aiden. And it's even better than I ever could have dreamed. His lips are soft, warm, and his kiss is gentle, tender, but soon his lips push more urgently against mine. He holds my face, and I slide my arms around him, and, somehow, I already knew what he'd taste like: winter, spring, summer, and fall, every season wrapped into one perfect everlasting moment.

Until I hear someone calling, "Aiden! There you are!"

16

AIDEN

I feel Emma groan just a tiny bit. Feel, because her mouth is open against mine, and the groan sends vibrations throughout my entire body. I lean farther into the kiss, but Emma gently pulls back. She's looking at something behind me, and before I have time to wonder what has ended the first and best kiss of my life, Grandma says, "Okay, you two, that's enough of that."

I close my eyes, willing Grandma to leave, or to at least come back later, but Emma says weakly, "Hi, Mrs. Gallo."

I open my eyes, turn, and say, "Grandma! Why are you here?"

"Last time I checked I live in Briar Glen, same as you."

"Yes, but here?" I swoop my arm through the air, gesturing at the park, then let my hand rest against the side of Emma's head.

Emma puts her hand on my hand, and she's smiling, and I'm smiling.

"You weren't answering your phone. Your dad and grandpa are

swamped and need your help." Grandma takes in the scene, sees how close Emma and I are sitting, and says, matter-of-factly, "Sorry to interrupt anything, but business is business."

She strides away, and I'm expected to follow her, like always.

I look at Emma, embarrassed and disappointed, but I can't stop grinning. Emma is grinning, too, and I think how just a few seconds ago I was kissing her. *I was kissing Emma!*

Emma touches my face, and I lean my head against her touch.

"Let's go!" Grandma says.

Emma rests her forehead against mine and says, "Go! I'll meet you at Cup o' Jo when you're done."

"That'll probably be after Cup o' Jo closes!" Grandma calls.

"How does she still have such good hearing?" I ask.

Emma keeps laughing, though, and says, "I'll see you tomorrow morning?"

"Yes!" I say, standing up.

"Great. It'll be the first morning of many."

Emma's lips are pink with the cold, and I force myself to tear my eyes away from her.

I walk to the car in a daze, pulling my sled, Mack trailing me.

"Sorry about that," Grandma says as Mackerel and I get in the car.

"It's okay." My head buzzes.

She loves me? She loves me! I begin to understand Sam's actions.

You're not good enough for her. Turns out, he was talking about himself.

We get to a stop sign, and Grandma turns to me. "So I guess you don't need any more space from Emma, huh?"

I grin. "Yeah, I guess you could say that."

"Told you."

"Told me what?"

"Everything," she says. She winks, and for the first time ever, I don't hate winks.

Grandma wasn't kidding about Dad and Grandpa being busy at the market, and they're both so relieved to see me. I immediately help customers shop, then ring and pack up sales, but my mind is somewhere else in Briar Glen. With Emma.

At one point while I stand next to Dad helping him wrap up a sale, he says, "I don't think I've ever seen you so happy to be at work."

"I don't think I've ever *been* so happy. Anywhere."

Dad raises an eyebrow. "Does this have anything to do with our chat the other day?"

"It does. But please don't make me talk about it?" I say with a chuckle.

I feel Dad looking at me out of the corner of my eye, but he turns back to the sale he's ringing up, and we work in happy silence the rest of the afternoon.

When I get home, I want to go to bed so it can be the next morning already. I feel like I used to the night before Christmas when I was a little kid. In my room, I pick up my phone. I open to the last text Emma sent me.

I'm here.

The next morning, I wake up as the sun peeks over the horizon. It's a little after seven. Emma and I didn't say what time we'd meet.

Mackerel wearily lifts his head from his dog bed, and I say, "It's okay, you can go back to sleep."

I get dressed quickly, my hands shaking, wishing I could somehow get ready faster.

The walk to Cup o' Jo is short, but it seems to take hours. Briar Glen is quiet. The snow makes everything so clean, so peaceful. I look again at the Snoopy decorations as I walk. I can't help but smile. And then I think: *She loves me.*

I get to Main Street, see all the lights my family has been hanging up for years. The Christmas tree that I've seen get lit every year of my life. The gazebo where Santa sat, when I finally was able to talk to him in second grade. It's all the same, but I'm not. Emma was right: Briar Glen isn't going anywhere. Maybe I am, though. Or maybe I'm not. Either way, Briar Glen will always be the place my family comes from.

The place I come from.

I open the door to Cup o' Jo. There are a few customers, and I see Jo busy behind the counter, but it's like they're all part of some fuzzy backdrop. Because I see Emma, two peppermint hot chocolates on the table in front of her. The drinks are still steaming.

"Hi," Emma says standing up slowly. "I know it's complicated because I go to school in New York, and we're best friends, but . . ." She's talking fast, avoiding eye contact. "You feel like home. Even though I don't really know where home is for me right now. But my heart knows. My heart is with your heart. Always. You're there, no matter what." She looks up at me.

"I love you," I say simply. It feels so good and so natural to say to her, and I feel myself grinning, and she's grinning. I take a step toward her.

"I love you," she says. She takes a step even closer to me. I smell the peppermint on her breath. My hands feel warm, and I look down. Emma is holding them. Emma is what makes me warm.

Emma leans close to me. I brush my lips against hers. I never could have dreamed how delicious she would taste.

She kisses me harder, and I know I'll never be cold again.

NEW YEAR'S EVE

Cup o' Jo is packed with people drinking sparkling cider. Everyone excitedly chats over the music, which is a mix of Christmas songs and different versions of "Auld Lang Syne."

The fireplace at the back of the shop roars, and Aiden and Emma sit in front of it, curled up together. Their mugs of peppermint hot chocolate sit on the table in front of them.

"Is it too late to make a New Year's resolution?" Aiden asks Emma as he strokes her wrist. How has he never realized that her wrists are beautiful?

Emma checks the time on her watch. "You have three more minutes." She snuggles up closer to Aiden, leaning her head against his shoulder. She can't believe how perfectly she fits.

"I work best under pressure," Aiden says.

"So it better be a good resolution!"

Aiden laughs. "Well, that was easy."

Emma lifts her head and looks at him expectantly.

"I resolve to never go six months without hearing your voice."

Emma sputters, "Six *months*?"

"Six *days*! Not even a whole week!"

"Six days?"

"Because you're overseas helping a nonprofit win a case and you don't have cell service. Or you've finally made it to Antarctica."

"Maybe you won't have to wait six days to talk to me because you'll be with me on one of these adventures?" Emma says, lightly elbowing Aiden. "Only if you want, though."

"Emma, I don't need to go to some faraway continent. Every day I've spent with you, every day I've known you, is the best adventure of my life."

Emma beams with brightness.

"Can I add another resolution?" Aiden asks.

Emma slowly nods her head, brighter than the stars.

"Well, I guess it's not a resolution, but may I visit you in New York?"

"I thought you'd never ask."

They lean toward each other, about to kiss, but Jo says, "Not yet, you two!"

Emma and Aiden reluctantly pull apart.

"Everyone! Quiet down!" Jo shouts over the din of joyful, happy chatter. "It's almost time to start the countdown!"

The coffee shop erupts in applause as everyone gets ready to ring in the new year. Lucy and Jack snake their way through the crowd.

Lucy holds a tray of cups of sparkling apple cider.

Emma and Aiden look at the tray uncertainly.

"I know, it's not peppermint hot chocolate," Jack chimes in from behind Lucy, his hand resting on Lucy's back.

He winks at Aiden, and Aiden finally knows how to return a wink—with a smile.

"Let me guess, maybe next time?" Lucy teases.

"Yep. I think we'll stick with our hot chocolate," Emma says, as Aiden leans forward for his mug.

"Happy New Year," Lucy says over her shoulder as she and Jack hand out drinks.

"Happy New Year!" Emma and Aiden say together.

Aiden gives Emma her mug, and they both take big gulps.

"Okay, here we go!" Jo shouts. "Ten . . . nine . . . eight . . ."

"Wait!" Aiden says, realization striking him. "You never told me *your* resolution, Emma Sherman!"

"Seven . . . six . . five . . ."

"That's easy, Aiden Cooper-Gallo."

"Four . . . three . . ."

"I resolve to be right here," Emma says. "With you."

"Two . . . one . . . HAPPY NEW YEAR!"

And with that, the year ends, and the next one begins, with a pepperminty kiss.

ACKNOWLEDGMENTS

Thank you, readers, for making a trip to Briar Glen with me, whether it be your first or second visit. I hope the book was as cozy an escape for you to read as it was for me to write. Thank you, librarians, booksellers, and teachers. The importance of your work cannot be stated enough.

Orlando Dos Reis, this is our fourth book together, and you continue to amaze me with your fun ideas, wise edits, and keen eye—thank you. Leni Kauffman, you once again brought my characters to life beautifully, and Stephanie Yang, I'm delighted to have another cover and book designed by you. Thank you also to Mary Kate Garmire, Cindy Durand, Priscilla Eakeley, Cady Zeng, Jael Fogle, and the entire Scholastic production department. Thank you as well, David Levithan, and to the sales, marketing, and publicity teams, especially Abby Jordan, for everything you've done to promote my books.

Thank you to my family, as always. I write for them, and

I write because of them. To Nick, for taking over any and all household duties without complaint while I wrote. To Mila, for all your name ideas, for your fact-checking, for being you. To Mom, Cosmo, Greg, Erin, for your unwavering encouragement, and love. And to Mary, Nicole, Lisa, Loren, Keith, Aaron, and Whitneigh; Dawn, Bob, Natalie; Gene, Susan, Chris, and Gina; Robin, Roman, Alex, Francesca, Katia, Mary, and Victor; Zen and Summer; Kevin and Mary Jo; the Casads; Kate, Tim, Meghan, Chris, Molly, Rob. How lucky I am that you're all part of my family. To Frank, Barb, and Nancy—we miss you.

My treatment group at Memorial Sloan Kettering Cancer Center continues to be an integral part of my life. Dr. Wang, Katie Rudy-Tomczak, Jen Keller—thank you for (literally) keeping me alive.

Thank you, Beacon, for serving as an inspiration for Briar Glen. And thank you to my friend and writing community in Beacon and beyond: Mary, Stephanie, Jessie, Liz, Laura, Nico, Billy, Oriane, Heather, Rebecca, Tricia, Rudha, Doug, Linda, Elise, Caiming, Beth, Charlie, Sarah, Emily, Devon, Ryan, Carolyn, Katie, Marianne, Stella, Kellie, Colm, Elizabeth, Dan, Claribel, Christy, Lindsey, Trish, Betsy, Dawn, Donna, Kim, Jane, Jen, Lauren O'Neill-Butler, Lavina, Amanda, Pearl, Lauren Biggs, Nathan, Chad, Kristen, Lucky, Rachel Losh,

Tyler, Rachel Parekh De Azua, Autumn, and Anna.

Finally, thank you, ARF Beacon, especially Amanda; Pets Alive; the North Shore Animal League; and the Humane Society of Pinellas, for introducing me to my rescue pets. And one more huge thank-you: to the ASPCA, Humane World for Animals, and all other animal rescue and shelter groups, for all the lives you've saved.

ABOUT THE AUTHOR

Katie Cicatelli-Kuc is the author of *Pumpkin Spice & Everything Nice*, among other young adult novels, and an assorted collection of books for young readers. She lives in a town not unlike Briar Glen in New York's Hudson Valley with her family and her animals. Check out her website, katiecicatelli.com, or follow her on Instagram at @katie_cicatelli_writes.